Large Print Eas
Easton, Robert Olney.
To find a place : Western

# To Find A Place

## Western Stories

# To Find A Place

**Western Stories**

## Robert Easton

**Thorndike Press • Chivers Press**
**Thorndike, Maine USA   Bath, England**

This Large Print edition is published by Thorndike Press, USA and by Chivers Press, England.

Published in 2000 in the U.S. by arrangement with Golden West Literary Agency.

Published in 2000 in the U.K. by arrangement with Golden West Literary Agency.

U.S.  Hardcover  0-7862-2781-8  (Western Series Edition)
U.K.  Hardcover  0-7540-4281-2  (Chivers Large Print)
U.K.  Softcover   0-7540-4282-0  (Camden Large Print)

*Acknowledgments may be found on page 267.*

The text of this Large Print edition is unabridged.
Other aspects of the book may vary from the original edition.

Set in 16 pt. Plantin by Al Chase.

Printed in the United States on permanent paper.

**British Library Cataloguing-in-Publication Data available**

**Library of Congress Cataloging-in-Publication Data**

Easton, Robert Olney.
    To find a place : Western stories / Robert Easton.
        p.    cm.
    ISBN 0-7862-2781-8 (lg. print : hc : alk. paper)
    1. Western stories.  2. Large type books.  I. Title.
PS3509.A7575 T6   2000
813'.52—dc21                                        00-042574

# Table Of Contents

# FOREWORD

My short fiction set in California and the
West is collected here for the first time in one
volume. Most of these stories originally ap-
peared in magazines as diverse as *The Atlantic
Monthly*, *Argosy*, *Collier's*, and *Esquire*. Sev-
eral also appeared in anthologies such as The
Modern Library's GREAT TALES OF
THE AMERICAN WEST (1945) and THE
MORROW ANTHOLOGY OF GREAT
WESTERN SHORT STORIES (1997). All
of them represent my enduring love and fas-
cination for Western America, and they are
in effect a prelude to my ongoing Saga of Cal-
ifornia series of novels about my native state,
THIS PROMISED LAND (1982), POWER
AND GLORY (1989), BLOOD AND
MONEY (1998), and the forthcoming
LOVE AND DESTINY, all of which sprang
from these same roots.

All of us try to find our place in life. These
stories helped me find mine. I hope they
may speak to you in that spirit.

Robert Easton
Santa Barbara, California

# TO FIND A PLACE

On a Saturday morning in September a man drove a small, out-of-date coupé along a county road bordering some yellow California hills. The road humped slightly every so often where the slopes had washed and fanned off into a long plain, flat as a pan, that ran away westward toward salt marshes and a bay. The name of the man doesn't matter — call him "I" if you like. But he was young, a stranger in these parts, and looking for his first job.

It was a few minutes before one o'clock when I caught the scent of many animals, mixed with the pleasant and exciting smell of sea wind over the summer ground, and topped the last hump in the road and saw the feed yards of El Dorado Investment Company, and all its thirteen thousand white-faced cattle cooped in pens like city blocks that spread away for miles clear to the river and the yellow fields bordering it.

At a sign with a great hand pointing, I turned and drove to a small box of a building that said — **OFFICE** — and here I inquired of a sleepy bookkeeper when Mr.

Archibald Jacks, the foreman, could be expected. The answer was one o'clock, at the barn, and the barn was over there two hundred yards where all the cattle began.

While the bookkeeper was talking, I let my eye wander a little — since this was the office of the largest enterprise of its kind in Western America, I wanted to have a look — and on the panel of an inner door I saw — **T. S. Ordway, Private**. I thought about it as I drove away. T. S. Ordway was a name known to most people west of the Rockies. He didn't raise cattle; he manufactured them. He turned beef into dollars as fast as Henry Ford turned cars off the assembly line. Three months in his yards and the heifer yearlings that had come so poor, so cheap, were shipped away as sleek as seals with half their added pounds clear profit. And he had steers, too, and canner cows and baloney bulls and anything that wore horns and a hide. He didn't care. "Give me the cattle ninety days," he used to say, "and I'll not have to brand 'em. They'll take the look o' the El." By which he meant his brand was the Rocking E L and his cattle stuffed so hard with good white fat that butchers who knew never bothered coming to see the animals they wanted; they simply telephoned and said — "Tom, I need a load

10

of heifers to average eight-seventy-five." — just as you would order so many pairs of shoes from a catalogue.

So I went along into that wilderness of boards and cattle where everything was strange, and stopped, and left the car, and stood beside a fence not too near the door of the barn nor yet too far away, but just between — about the place I thought correct for a young man who didn't have a job but hoped to get one.

Trucks were going by — big semi-trailers full of hay, partitioned in the middle like orange boxes. They sang past me down the road, and I saw the flash of the sun-and-wind-burned faces with whom I was to work; and my own face got red, and my clothes didn't fit, and the chromium on my old coupé, which I had taken such scrupulous care of these past five years, looked as bright and silly as French doors on a barn. Trucks and more trucks passed, flat-beds, diesels — every kind, in pairs, in convoys, disappearing toward some secret destination in the heart of Thomas Ordway's city, where the warehouses and mill rose like castles of galvanized iron, and a gigantic pit for beet pulp, wide as a stadium, filled the air with a sour, sticky smell. An arm of the river, a man-made slough, reached in here, and barges were tied close against a dock, and giant cranes moved over them, nodding and whirling as they bit and lifted and spat away the pulp to empty the barges and fill the pit.

From everywhere there rose the sounds of action — of belts and wheels, frictions, grindings, loadings, and liftings and all the business of a morning — till even the air you breathed was busy, and I could see the sweat of working men soak through their shirts between the shoulder blades. Still no foreman came. If anyone had handed me a hoe and said — "Here, go to work!" — I would have considered myself far richer than T. S. Ordway.

About then somebody did come, a man in a dusty pickup who stopped his little truck five steps away and slumped immediately behind the wheel and began picking his teeth with a match. He had a short face, brown and wrinkled as a nut, sharp as a rodent's, and he wore an ancient cattleman's hat. He stuck both thumbs under the bib of his overalls and stared at the horizon, while the match worked itself across his mouth and back again.

"You Mister Jacks?" I asked.

"Part of the time," said the man, looking far away. His attention veered slightly to the southwest. He began singing in a flat nasal voice — "O Susanna, don't you cry for me. . . ." — but broke off suddenly and said, looking due south: "You the new man?"

I said I was.

Archibald Jacks hummed another bar.

"They's a boy inside the barn'll show ye what to do," he popped out all together and at the same time was stricken into action, dropped his song, spat out his match, started his pickup, and drove away.

In the doorway of the barn I met a little man all in blue denim, so bowlegged you could have put a half-grown hog between his knees and never got his blue jeans dirty.

"Howdy," said the little man. He led a saddled horse, and he leveled at me a pair of eyes like two revolvers.

I said — "Howdy." — quickly . . . the first time I remember ever using the word, and somehow it sounded like an echo to "Hands up!"

Yet the little man was not unfriendly. He had heard of me; he would show me my horse. "Barb's a gentle horse," he said, leading the way down the barn, behind the mangers. "Pretty good cow horse, too, for this part of the country." He pointed to a chunky sorrel with white stockings. "Looks more like the ponies we had back home."

"Where was that?" I asked.

"Utah," said the little man. "Guess Utah was the last one I had. Say, what do they call you?"

I told him my name, and the little man put his hand out and said: "Mine's Dynamite."

"Danny?" I said.

"No," he said, quite seriously, *"Dynamite."* He was adjusting a stirrup for me. "Never did give a damn for twisted stirrup leathers," he said. "Never did see 'em till I come to Californy. Or Oregon. Guess Oregon was first . . . I'd rode for this feller quite some time . . . Charlie Devers . . . Ringbolt Charlie, we called him. I'd noticed once before his leathers was twisted, but I just figured, you know, that they'd *got* twisted, and he'd straighten 'em when he had the chance. So one day we was riding for White River to do something . . . I forget what just now, to see a feller who had horses or something . . . anyhow, we'd got us down the road a spell and broke our ponies to a lope and I noticed them leathers o' Charlie's still was twisted. 'Hey,' I hollers, 'your leathers!' Charlie, he cranes first over this side, then over that, and looks and gets darker in the face with looking, till I knowed his thunder was a-gonner roll. 'Twisted?' he says. 'Boy, *you're* telling *me* them leathers is twisted? Now what the hell is the matter with you? How do you think leathers orter be?' Oh, he'd got kindy flusterated, took him clear to White River to cool out . . . and then I explained how back home all the leathers was hung straight. See, he'd never heard o' my way, and I'd never heard of his'n, but I guess that's the way it is in life . . . they's a heap of things a feller never hears about till he travels and meets other folk but his own."

Dynamite made a little boy's grin. He had animal teeth, very white and sharp. "That's how you'll be here," he said, slapping the rump of Barb, the chunky sorrel, "meetin' other folk but your own. So let's start now and get acquainted."

He led the way outside.

Dynamite rode a ragged bay that was the very meaning of the word nag, all head and hind end, and, when he was aboard, he showed me how his stirrups hung freely so that he could rake a bronc' with his spurs from its ears to its hips. Then he took off down an asphalt road, where Barb and I got just three feet of clearance from the whining trucks, like any other vehicle, and finally we turned into a side alley between mangers lined with cattle, where the feeding heads made a solid row of white almost within

15

touching of my stirrup. The Herefords hardly raised an eye to watch us pass. This, said Dynamite, was because a feed truck had just dumped its load. He said ten of them took all day to feed the yards, that each lot of cattle was given a number and a pen when it came in, and thereafter was never moved until ready to cut and ship, that a good heifer might gain three pounds a day while a steer put on two, but she-stuff brought a cent less per pound because they had more waste to them. "Take these ladies here, three-sixty-fours . . . we're shipping on 'em now. See that roan by the water trough, how the fat fits tight along her back and covers her hip bones and makes them like pads aside her tail? See that satchel down in front between her legs? That's what you eat when you eat boiled brisket. . . . Now, lookie here, alongside these here ones over here, three-sixty-nines . . . they just come in last week. Both are long yearlings, both good Hereford, but these on this side is just a-commencin' to eat. See the bellies on 'em? If a critter don't belly down thataway first, she won't never get fat."

Dynamite pointed out the different brands, all famous through the West, the Open-A-Bar, the S Q, Double Slash, and 3 C — each speaking for a country and a people like the flags of ships met in a harbor. One came from Stovepipe out of Amarillo, one from West Texas, one from Oklahoma prairie, and the plains of Oregon. Each stood for its great name — Pecos, Río Grande, Houston, and Tombstone — for running irons, dust and leather, and range fires by the rimrock. "They'd take a lot of tellin', them brands," said Dynamite, "but to make it easy old T. S. Ordway put 'em in a pen and just called 'em three-sixty-nines."

The cattle ate an evil-smelling mash that had something like gold dust scattered over it. I asked what this might be, and Dynamite said the mash was pulp left from the processing of sugar beets, and the dust was dry-feed from El Dorado's mill, where oat and barley hay were chopped with vetch and alfalfa and mixed with grain and milo maize, cottonseed cake, molasses, bone meal rich in phosphorous, and one or two other ingredients that made the best meal a cow critter ever ate and that laid the fat on thick and hard and white as cream. The exact proportion only T. S. Ordway knew. It was his discovery, his secret, and on it he had built his El Dorado. "He ain't no cattleman . . . hell, he's a businessman. Why, all of this place ain't no more than a drawer in his desk. He owns ranches from here to Mexico, banks, buildings in Los Angeles and San Francisco . . . everything a man can own. But he knows land best. It was land brought him here." Dynamite swept the western horizon with his arm. "Twenty thousand acres of the richest land in America. Sure, it was under water, half of it, when he come. Give him credit. He done her, he made her, and she's all his."

I looked into the wind that filled my eyes with Thomas Ordway's golden feed, whipped from the mangers, and saw it coming on the yellow fields up from salt marshes and the bay.

"Some panoramic, eh?" said Dynamite.

In the sunlight the sloughs wound through the reeds like threads of silver. Gulls and water-birds were dark motes, floating high, shining white suddenly when they tipped against the sun. Beyond them the river spread to make a bay, and far in the distance was again compressed by hills. I let my eye follow the compass around. South across the water was a fringe of little towns so far away their houses looked like pebbles on the opposite shore. Eastward along the yards low harvest hills unfolded to the river, with here and there a flock of sheep like a cluster of gray aphids. Northward for many miles the great alluvial plain rose gradually until it met the hills from which it had come; and, everywhere beyond, more hills rolled northward as far as a man might see, holding in their hollows clumps of un-painted farm buildings that looked as if they were dying there slowly, like bits of wood in the trough of the sea. And all of these hills were such a color of gold and had in them such a marvelous grace of line that, when you looked steadily, they seemed to move, as though they might have flowed once from the same source and instantly been stilled.

"She's big, is El Dorado," said Dynamite, "and famous, but she has her faults like the rest of us. Some things you'll like, some not. Jacks, he's a good boss . . . the work ain't hard . . . the fellers of the best. But you'll wonder at seven working days a week and nights when they need you to unload cattle, and three bucks for a day. But we have a good time. We got to. . . . You will, too, when you're 'quainted around. Go up to Bird Town payday, come to our dances . . . say, we're having one tonight, and you can come. Ever square-dance? All we need's a fiddle and a bare floor, none o' this here fox-trot shilly-shally."

A truck that looked like a cigar box high on a frame was coming down the alley, spewing beet pulp out one side and leaving just enough room for a very thin horse to pass if he had steady nerves. Perched on a rear platform was a man who regulated the speed of unloading and called to the cattle in the pens who followed him, bucking and bawling with delight. I followed Dynamite and threw my reins away, let old Barb take me past the truck with nearly an inch to spare between my right knee and the steel frame. Dynamite was already in conversation with the man on the rear platform whose name was Whitey and who, all the time he talked, was kicking a lever with his foot and poking at the pulp with a big feed fork and interrupting himself now and then to cry out something in a high voice nobody could understand but which meant that the driver was to move on. Dynamite and I came slowly behind.

"Goin' to the dance?"

"Shore 'nuff."

"You wasn't to the last one."

"Shore was."

"Like hell."

"*Shore* I was . . . I'd go to a dance even if there was nobody there but me."

"I can believe it."

"No, I didn't go. Did you?"

"Yeah."

"How come?"

"Well, I figured you wasn't a-gonna be there."

"Oh, scairt, eh?"

And so it went for a hundred yards down the alley, until the pulp was all gone into the manger and Whitey gave a final cry and a wave to us and was whisked away for another load.

Whitey talked funny — not straight Western like Dynamite nor fully Southern, but something in between. For instance, he pronounced "wrench" and "ranch" exactly alike.

I asked where fellows came from who talked like that.

"Arkansas," said Dynamite. "Ain't you never heard a Arkansawyer talk? Well, you will. That's what we got here, along with the Okies and Missourians, and some from Texas. But you can tell a Arkansawyer. Mostly he's long and thin, red-cheeked and full of big old lies. Great hands to talk, they are, and to throw stones, and every one that's rode a horse says he's a cowboy. Like Jacks . . . he's one, but he ain't no cowboy. He's just a Arkansas farm boy growed up into a good job, and fat cattle is all he knows. Okies, they's different. We ain't got many that's gen-u-ine, but one bunch lives up to Bird Town that I'll show ye, a whole county of 'em . . . Grandad, old Mammy, Pap and Ma, married boys and their kids . . . all junked together in one room. You couldn't miss 'em. They all got long manes and that drawed-up look, and wear them Okie caps like they was a-gonna drive a train some place."

"I said California people didn't care much for Okies. There's been a lot of hard words said about them and a lot written."

"Well," said Dynamite, "I tell you . . . I-tell-you-how-it-is. Take a sack of beans out of the field . . . any kind, pink, white, no matter . . . and pour 'em in a kettle and see how the foul stuff always comes on top . . . the straws and little stones. Same way with people. Pour your state into mine and it's the foul stuff shows up most, but the good beans is underneath there just the same, only a feller don't see 'em right away. Shucks sakes, we all got poor white trash . . . Utah, California, New York City . . . all of us. Taint nothing to git flusterated over. . . . These folk here, they's good beans, not trash. Maybe they had a place back home, but the dust got it, or maybe they got brothers and sistern 'n' enough back there to care for the old folks, and they has to git out and rustle for theirselves. . . . Sure . . . ," said Dynamite, and then his eye wandered quickly and he shouted: "Hey you, Will Ragan, what kind of janitor's work are ye up to this day?"

A man bending over a water trough in one of the pens straightened up slowly and revealed a shaggy Irish face on which three days' growth of beard lay like a heavy frost. "The work o' lazy cowboys is what I'm up to this day," said William Ragan, folding his hands across the top of a broom he had been using to clean the trough and getting ready to enjoy himself.

"Now, lookie here, lookie here . . . ! I'll not have no talkin' smart on such a day!" said Dynamite, and they both laughed and laughed. "Say, what did ye think of the fight?" Dynamite meant the prize fight of the night before in which a Pittsburgh Irishman had nearly whipped Joe Louis for the world's heavyweight title.

"Oh, aye," said William, "and it's well enough, I guess. Or else the Irish would be a-thinkin' themselves better than the niggers." And again he roared and slapped his thigh and poked Dynamite's horse in the flank with his broom handle, and there was three minutes' general rampage before Dynamite and I could go on.

We passed a construction crew repairing an alley, and Dynamite got his little boy's

23

grin ready for each man and a word launched with the full vigor of his name: "Hi, Fred . . . hi, Jingle. Not doin' much, eh, Joe?" And to a man named Tex, leaning on a shovel: "*Care*-ful! Easy there, Tex, or ye're a-gonner bust that handle!" He called them all the WPA and cursed them, and they loved it.

Then for a while Dynamite had nothing to say, so he sang a song:

**O send me a letter,**
**send it by mail.**
**Send it in care *of***
**the Birmingham jail.**
**The Birmingham jail, love.**
**The Birmingham jail.**
**The Birmingham jail.**
**Pining for you, love . . .**

On a space of level ground we passed a haystack three hundred feet long and thirty high where a crane unloaded semi-trailers of hay. The trucks drove alongside the stack; the crane swung over, dangling a cable to which the driver hooked both ends of a net made of wire that lined the compartments of the truck and onto which the hay had been loaded. Five seconds later a parcel weighing several tons was delivered on the stack just as freight is loaded on a ship, there to be spread around by three men with pitchforks. "Old Ordway figured it," said Dynamite. "They tell how he come down here one afternoon and seen a dozen guys pitching hay and a dozen more trying to catch what the wind didn't blow away, and then he set and went to thinkin' and next Tuesday-week he bought the company another crane and a hundred yards of wire cable and let a dozen men go down the road."

So we made our rounds until we came to the scale house by the mill where the men like to sit for a smoke in the shade, or go inside the little corrugated-iron shack and read the *True Detective*s Gene, the weigh master, keeps piled there under his scale. By four o'clock it's time for talking; so the boys were ready on the bench, when Dynamite and I came around. Then they shut up like clams and looked at the earth and the sky and somehow managed to see everything there was about me before I'd got within a hundred yards.

Dynamite sailed right in. "Jody," he said to a thin little man with glasses and a great big country hat of straw, "don't pay no 'tention to them other guys but just give me a plain answer . . . when do we run our race?"

"Any time suits me," said Jody, making marks on the ground with the used end of a match.

"OK, then," said Dynamite, "tomorry. We'll run tomorry instead of going to church. We'll measure out one hundred yards of the road this side o' Bird Town."

"You want to make a man work Sunday?" said Jody.

"*Chicken!*" said a young man who lounged out of the scale house and was able to keep both hands in his pockets by nudging the screen with one elbow and letting it slam shut behind. "Jody, he's made ye a play. Ante or throw in your hand." Jaydee Jones, raised on Arkansas corn fritters, ham, and hominy, had at one time or other taken something dark inside him that came out now on his face and made every word he said funny, with a sting. Not looking anywhere in particular, he sauntered over to Dynamite and began combing his horse's mane with the fingers of one hand. He asked if there was a dance that night, if Lear had paid Dynamite the two bucks. Then Jaydee's face got serious with thought. "Say," he said, "did you hear about that 'lectrician over at Vista City?"

"What about him?" said Dynamite.

"Dead," said Jaydee.

"Yeah?" said Dynamite.

For a minute, then another minute and another that was all.

"How did it happen?" I asked.

Jaydee said quickly: "Oh, he set down on a fruit cake and a currant ran up his laig."

The only sound was a muffled rubbing of the gears inside the mill. Jaydee sauntered back and leaned against the wall of the scale house and called for somebody inside named Pringle to bring him out the Climax Plug.

"Well," Dynamite said to me, "the hell with these guys. We got important business to attend to. Let's get outta here."

We rode away, and, when I saw Dynamite watching me, I grinned for the little cowboy and said: "I was cut too green, wasn't I? Bet if you'd stick me in the ground, I'd grow."

"Aw, shucks," said Dynamite. "You ate horse, sure. But we all got to sometimes. Now you'll know Jaydee . . . he's kindy thataway."

We rode the alley toward the barn, watching for leaky troughs or boards off gates, dead animals, or any of those casual changes the laws of chance occurrence bring wherever a species is gathered. We found only Jacks, sitting in his pickup by the barn as though he just happened to be there,

27

sucking a match and looking at the horizon. In a voice so confidential it would have served to announce the merger of six companies he told Dynamite the cattle trucks would be in at eleven.

When he had gone, Dynamite swore all around the compass. "Never knew it to fail . . . *never* did. Cattle, cattle every day in the week, and, if a feller wants to dance Saturday night and have a little fun, it's nothing doing, it's *cattle*. Jesus Christ. I quit."

He stormed into the barn.

He was still saying — "To hell with 'em . . . I quit." — when the ponies were bedded down and I was driving toward the buildings of the main ranch. "Lemme out here," said Dynamite as we passed a quadrangle of galvanized iron garages, the place the feed trucks stayed all night.

"You're not going to the bunkhouse?" I asked.

"Me? Hell, no. What would I want with a bunkhouse. I got one o' my own up to Bird Town. Wife and four kids in it." Dynamite lifted himself out, then reached for his lunch bucket. "I'll call for ye at eleven," he said, still angry, and walked away.

To reach the bunkhouse of El Dorado Investment Company, you passed a kind of used car lot where no vehicle built within

28

the last ten years, with any paint, upholstery, unbroken window, or any kind of op-
erating decency was exhibited. The
bunkhouse itself was two old farm houses
sewn together with some sketchy
carpentering. There were in all about a
dozen bare rooms — six beds in the front
one and so on back. Over a kind of closet by
the door someone had smeared **Bull Cook**
in red paint. I knocked here, and an old man
came out and pointed to a bed in the corner
beside what once had been a chiffonier.
"Give the mattress a once-over," he said,
handing me the fly spray. "Washroom's out
back. The Widder Ellen, we call it, is that
house by the cypress tree."

I worked over the mattress, then dumped
my blankets on the bed and took a towel and
went to find the washroom. Men coming
from work lined the sink. There were gray
basins and hot and cold running water. In
the confusion it was easy to come and go,
and I might have moved unnoticed but for
the electrician who had sat upon the fruit
cake. I read knowledge of this unhappy
story in every face and fled away indoors,
devoured by a thousand eyes. I spent the
time till supper lying on my bed because
there was no place to sit except a bench and
table in the middle of the room, where a

man might expect to sit when he had worked for El Dorado at least a year and never asked questions out of turn.

The occupants of the other beds came in. You would find them repeated over and over in any bunkhouse of the West, men of indefinite age, the old jaspers who drive the Chevies and Model-A Fords, who lift the picks and build the fences, whose only home is four bare walls and a bare floor.

The supper bell rang before it was time to light two bulbs that hung on cords from the ceiling. Nobody had said a word.

I followed behind the men, under cypress trees where the wind touched mournfully, into the cookhouse where all the others found seats. The long table was set with white oilcloth and heavy white plates and dishes heaping with food. Through an open door was the kitchen; the cook stood over his black stove, and rows of pots and spoons and knives hung each from its nail. In the doorway lounged a great gob of a man who wore a sailor's hat and nothing over his undershirt and pants but an apron. He smiled stupidly at everyone, his teeth protruding, and, when I told him I was a new hand, said — "Sure, sure!" — and laid one greasy paw across my back and pointed with the other to the end of the table.

There were boiled spuds and fat red beans that would keep a man going all day long, and pale string beans that really were strung, and also meat done country-style, to the color and texture of gray leather. At intervals along the table stood those mysterious clumps of sauces, bottles that are never used or cleared away but stand forever fixed to the tables of American ranches — a sort of nucleus around which meals are built.

I carefully did not ask for things beyond my reach for fear of drawing attention, but the men were too busy to look at me. Along the table the double row of bodies bent and went to eating with a deadly earnest, hunched forward, no two alike yet all the same, each scarred and twisted, grown crooked from the roots, too long for its trunk or too short for its head, here missing a thumb, here an eye; yet all of them had grown in spite of every difficulty, like tough cedar trees from a rock.

Except for the Arkansawyers, the eaters were silent. But these were so altogether friendly they just couldn't stand to see a bite go down alone; it had to have a word for company, or maybe two. And if three were needed and your mouth was full of potatoes, that didn't matter — it just showed

31

what a good man could do with the English language. "Jody," said Jaydee Jones, "pass me the Mussolini."

Jody handed over a platter of red spaghetti.

"You backed out today," said Jaydee. "Jody, you got feather-legged."

"Aw, you're just a-talkin' now," said Jody.

"Diney offered ye the chance . . . ye wouldn't run."

"Let's me and *you* run," said Jody.

"Me run ag'in' you? Why man," said Jaydee, "I'd tromp you to death in fifty yards."

"Let's make it a hundred then," said Jody. "I sure wanna live till payday."

"Hell, I run down a deer oncet," went on Jaydee.

"That's nothing," Jody said. "Look at Roy there. He run down a Arkansas woman."

Everybody did look at Roy who got about the color of the spaghetti.

"Sure," said Jaydee, "and ever since he ain't been able to buy her a pair of shoes."

The fat waiter wanted to be friends. While everybody still was laughing at Roy, he called from the doorway to Jaydee: "Jaydee, hey Jaydee! Let's you and me go to Sacramento this Saturday. I know a couple of dolls up there on G Street." Most of all the fat waiter wanted to be acquainted with a man named Sandy, who sat back toward him on the near side of the table. Whenever possible, he stood close to Sandy, watching him dumbly like an affectionate dog. He brought freshly filled platters with — "Here Sandy, try this . . . ?" — or — "Here Sandy, this'll put lead in your pencil." When Sandy talked about wild parties with the man next to him, the fat waiter eagerly broke in: "Did you ever throw a whing-ding in Chicago?" But Sandy kept on talking and after a while the waiter had to make his own answer, grinning at the air: "Boy, I sure did in 'Thirty-Six. I sure threw a hummer there!"

After supper, the men stacked their dishes and left them on the table by the kitchen door. Nobody smoked until he got outside and then within ten steps every man seemed to have rolled and lit a Bull Durham. They went in groups of three or four, laughing, swearing, tripping each other, ragging Jody about his foot race and Roy about his Arkansas woman, and, at intervals between them, walked a solitary figure, a stranger, an habitual grouch, a pervert, a Mexican, or some other outcast — each desiring in his heart nothing so much as to be included in these rough words and coarse laughter.

Someone had switched the lights on in the bunkhouse and lit a fire in the wood stove. The bare bulbs brought to completion the bare walls, ceiling, floors, and faces of the men, and made them into a little world of barrenness sealed by the night. They lay upon their beds, heads on folded hands, and stared at the ceiling until time to go to bed. Although it was hot and the place filled quickly with tobacco smoke, nobody opened a window. Nobody said a word. I slept.

The next I knew, Dynamite was standing over me, saying: "Come along, cowboy."

Outside it was bright starlight. The wind had risen, and darkness had released into it ten thousand new and exciting smells, each like a thought of voyages and adventure, and now it rose again and beat above us wildly through the trees like water on a lonely shore.

Dynamite's car was a 1926 Packard sedan, a monster vehicle, the kind wealthy ladies keep forever in their retinue, pensioned like faithful servants. But here the lady died too soon. Dynamite paid seventy-five dollars for the car, he said, and told how it came in handy as nursery for his children and as a truck for hauling wood or hogs or calves that were born in the yards and taken home. It had no glass in the rear door, no rear seat, no upholstery that a child or a hog had not stained and scented permanently, but wonderful to say — and this Dynamite pointed out immediately — the vases inside the rear doors that once a liveried chauffeur had filled with jasmine and gardenias were still unbroken, and in one of them were tucked brown shreds of flowers, poppies, placed there last spring by one of Dynamite's little girls.

Dynamite parked beside the barn, scrunched down, and kicked his feet up on the dashboard and told me to get in back, if I liked, because the trucks might be an hour or they might be five. Reluctantly I did so, climbing over from the front seat into I could not see what perils, and finally making myself almost comfortable between an old tire and a wad of gunny sacks that served as rear seat.

For a time nothing was said. The wind brought a cold mist up from the marshes that shut out the stars and set the foghorns moaning on the river. Across the road cattle stirred in their pens, coughing now and then, and the wind beside us made a lonely, lonely sound through the cracks in the barn.

"Oh, I hate this place!" said Dynamite. "Sometimes I hate it more than ever I did man or woman. Funny a feller can git so riled at just a place. But Jesus, seven days a week is wearisome, very wearisome. Last time I had off was in May to go to a rodeo . . . one day I took."

Again he was quiet, then flared up: "I and the wife had hell tonight. . . . Got home from work, nobody there, no bath, no supper, chickens into the tomatoes, back door open. Pretty soon, here they come, the whole dang chivaree and the dog, trailing in off the hill like a herd a-comin' to water. 'What the hell is it now?' I says to her. I was mad anyway, see, 'bout not gettin' to the dance. Well, it was the sow. The sow *this,* the sow *that* . . . *'the sow got restless so we let her out. . . .'* Well, the sow's gonna farrer, that's why she's restless, and I told that woman a thousand times not to let her out 'cause she'll hide her pigs sure as hell's fire, and we'll have fed her six months for nothing. So I was mad, and we went 'round and 'round. Me and the wife don't get along, anyway. Never did."

"You're from Utah," I said. "I thought people there had lots of wives and were always happy."

"No more, they don't . . . 'least not in public, but I knew old Mormons back in the Bookcliffs that by God never knowed they'd joined the United States. They done her the old way still . . . wives, kids, the whole she-bang. Oh, Mormons is good people. Take an outlaw traveling through their country . . . they'll always help him, never squeal on him."

"You're a Mormon?"

"Oh, kind of, I guess . . . kind of a Jack-Mormon. That was when I worked for one on Tennessee Crick out o' Rock City . . . old Josiah Bean. . . . Bear of a worker, old Joey was, and a devil of a good man with stallions. Had dozens of 'em. Some he'd caught wild out of the hills and some he'd raised, but they all was gentle when he come around. He taught me a lot about stallions. 'Never let 'em get away with nothin',' he says. 'A stallion's not like a gelding that'll try ye once and quit . . . he's cocky. He figures, if you win today, maybe he'll win tomorry, and he'll keep a-trying ye and keep a-trying.' I seen old Joey lead a black maverick stud through a barn full of mares, and, if old stud cocked an ear or made so much as a whicker under his breath, Joey'd turn and just kick the stuffin' outta him right under the belly where it hurts, and then he'd turn around and lead that stud back and forth two or three times more just to show him. Great guy, old Joey. . . . Used to talk the

Mormon religion to me. I was just a snot of a kid then, and I guess he figured he'd get me early and lead me in the blessed way. I'd sit there on a bale of hay and let my eyes get big as saucers when he'd talk about God and hellfire. Pretend to take it all, you know, but Joey had a little daughter sixteen years old . . . Letticia . . . Letticia Bean . . . that I took to more'n ever I did his preaching. I never could go that stuff about turn yer other cheek when a guy slaps ye on this one. . . . Could you?"

I said I'd found it hard to go sometimes.

"And that stuff about hellfire, how when a feller goes to hell and gets to burnin' he don't never burn up, just stays there forever and burns and burns. I can't see it. I can't see how any Lord Jesus is gonna be that cruel. Why, take even these here gangsters, John Dillingers and people, you wouldn't want to treat them that way, would ye? And tell *me* that just ordinary folks like you and me that does a sin or two is a-gonna burn and burn! *I* can't see it. . . . You got religion?"

"Kind of," I said. "My grandfather was a minister."

"Catholic?"

"No, Episcopal."

"A what?"

I explained about the Episcopal Church.

"My granddaddy was a Baptist," said Dynamite. "That's pretty near the same as a Christian, ain't it?"

I agreed, and Dynamite continued: "I had an Aunt Olga that was great on the Catholic Church . . . what I mean, she was for it strong! Used to say she'd give God Almighty anything she had, and I reckon she would. Uncle Willie was different. He was off somewheres most of the time, though he always did send money home, and every year or two he'd come back himself, and Olga would have another baby . . . nineteen she totaled. But she thought the world of Uncle Willie. Said she'd rather live with him in a dugout than with any other man in a castle, and that's about what she done. . . . Oh, that Uncle Willie was a great feller to hunt! One time I remember, he went to Canada and sent Aunt Olga home a moose, just the head of it, ye know. . . . Oh, I guess this here God business is all right, if ye like it . . . I just don't care for it myself."

I was sleeping again, when Dynamite sang out — "Here they be!" — and I heard the guttural roar of the diesel and saw the dark hull of truck-and-trailer turning toward the barn, cutting the fog with powerful searchlights and decorated fore and aft like a ship with red and yellow clearance lights. The monster shifted gears and roared on by to find the chute.

Dynamite was there before it, signaling the driver with his flashlight as the door came opposite the chute. Then he took the bull-board, a small beam four feet long and several inches wide fitted with iron cross-pieces at the end, and dropped it in the narrow gap between the chute and the truck. Then he undid and lifted out the door and wired it to the side of the chute. From inside came the stench of cattle. They were seen dimly, stowed like sacks in the darkness. They did not try to come out.

Dynamite climbed the top of the truck. The driver was standing by a headlight, looking at his watch.

"Hey there below!" shouted Dynamite.

"Hey there above!" shouted the driver. "Is that you, Powder Keg?"

"And who else might it be, will ye tell me that? And while ye are at it, tell me where ye've been this past hour and a half?"

"Whadya mean . . . where have I been? I been traveling, boy, traveling! Since eight o'clock this morning I've had my nose to that old concrete."

"Oh, don't hand me them stale pertaters. I know you guys . . . stop here for a steak, stop there for a beer, stop in Modesto to see my gal. . . ."

While he was talking, Dynamite kicked at the heads of the cattle nearest the door, and now he turned on them his full attention in words that lashed like cuts of rawhide. "Hyar, hyar ye sons-of-bitches! Outside!"

But the cattle were afraid of the open door.

"Shine your light in the chute," commanded Dynamite, and, when this was done, the cattle went right out. They were small cattle, yearlings, poor and weak. "Where did ye get *these* things?" said Dynamite.

"Oh, down the line there five hundred miles. . . . Havermeyers, isn't it? I got it on my book. First trip ever I made to that place."

"Bad road?"

"Bad road! No road at all. Blue cracked a drive shaft coming out and Dolly . . . no telling when Dolly'll be here."

"Never knew it to fail," said Dynamite.

The driver pulled ahead. The trailer was unloaded, and Dynamite and I took the cattle down the alley a hundred yards to the scales, Dynamite explaining that by order of the State Railroad Commission, which being a *railroad* commission naturally had it

41

in for trucks, all cattle trucks must weigh their loads immediately on reaching their destination, while for the railroads this was not true. "It's the old railroad graft, is what it is. They got their commission, see? And the trucks ain't got the chance of a snowball in hell."

The scales was a galvanized iron building at the end of the alley. You pushed the cattle clear down and then closed a gate which held them in the alley till you could go around and open the scale door and push the critters in, one draft at a time. Dynamite went ahead inside and lit an electric bulb, and I could hear him slapping the iron markers on the bar until they came in balance. "We'll take 'em half and half," the cowboy called, coming back, and we advanced together in the darkness and let the shapes of yearlings swirl around us toward the light until Dynamite leaped out, shouting terribly, which drove back half the bunch and sent the others nearly out the end of the scales. He slammed the heavy door just in time to stem the backwash of cattle, and I followed him into the region of the electric bulb, which was nothing but a bare dirt floor and a box that housed the weighing mechanism and a board that jutted from the wall and evidently served as desk, for there were two old notebooks on it and a pencil.

"Ye can count 'em off," said Dynamite, bending over and tapping the markers and saying — "Whoa, cattle, whoa, cattle." — in a voice designed to keep the tangled, swirling, bawling mass of cattle on the scale from destroying itself. I looked at the yearlings through a crack between two boards. The yellow light striped them weirdly. They didn't look at all poor or weak, and I wondered how any man on earth would be able to count them when that door came open.

"OK!" sang Dynamite.

I opened the door wide.

Nothing happened. Then one animal put a foot out; then it took a step; then an avalanche of cattle rattled out over the boards like stones rolling down a mountain.

"How many?" said Dynamite.

"Dunno," I said.

"Didn't think ye would," said Dynamite. "But that's OK . . . that's all right. Next time stand out front a little and they'll not go so fast."

"Yeah, that's all right," I said. "That's hell, that's *suicide!*"

Dynamite laughed and laughed.

The truck had rolled down opposite the scales and stopped, its great cylinders idling hoarsely, getting their breath after five hundred miles. The driver, known as Done Movin', the Laziest Man in the World, helped weigh the second draft.

"Not bad," said Dynamite. "Not bad for a city-bred."

"Listen, small man, I was punching cows before you was born," replied Done Movin', and stuck Dynamite affectionately with a pencil. He was a grinning man, fat, with bad teeth, and he wore brown whipcord trousers and khaki shirt and a chauffeur's cap on the back of his head with three Union buttons pinned to it.

Dynamite assailed him once more: "How'd you happen to git here first? Most times you piddle in 'long about the middle of next week." And they insulted each other back and forth, while Dynamite weighed the cattle and I waited by the door, wondering what it might be to stand in front of fourteen thousand, two hundred and twenty-eight pounds of terror-stricken beef.

Dynamite gave his OK.

I had the sudden inspiration not to open the door very wide, and then the cattle might pour out thinly like anything else. I cracked the door a few feet. A yearling nosed out suspiciously, another followed, and another was three, and then ten thousand yearlings hit the door and the door hit me and I went down against the fence and stayed there while the side of my head took fire slowly and the stars went around and around.

Dynamite poked his face out. "Hey cowboy? All right?" Then he saw me and began to laugh. Done Movin' came, and the moment he saw me his face brightened and he joined Dynamite in a truly hearty laugh. "Don't never stand *behind* a door thataway," said Dynamite. "You'll get killed. Open the thing wide and stand out front where they can see ye."

As I came back inside the scales, holding my head in a handkerchief, Done Movin' was reminded of a story: "Like the other day I had my racks off and went to hauling grain. So I had a flat right in front of that asylum there in Napa and got my tools out and went to work. D'rectly this guy come along, decent enough, 'bout fifty I'd say, could have been anybody's daddy, and he starts a-axing questions. Axed me what I done, and I told him. Axed me how much I had on, and I could tell him to a pound . . . thirty-one thousand, one hundred and eighty . . . 'cause I'd just weighed in at the Bridge. 'Thirty-one thousand,' he says, just as polite, and . . . 'Thank you,' . . . and he walks away. Well, I changed my tire and drove along and was gettin' in towards Napa when I heard the siren. 'Say,' the copper tells me, 'you run over a guy back there.' He's kindy severe. 'Nossir,' I says, 'I never run over nobody . . . not that I know of.' 'You come along with me,' he says. So we turn around together and go back, nine mile, maybe ten, and we get to the asylum and right there in front is the feller who'd been axing me them questions. He's kind of down and out . . . fact is he's plastered to the pavement like a postage stamp . . . a loony, see? He'd been trying to do it a long time, and, when he did get loose, he axed me all them questions so polite and then just walked around between the truck and trailer and laid down."

"Well, I'll be god damned," said Dynamite.

"Yes, sir," said Done Movin', "that's what happened. Here," he said, "sign my ticket. I gotta be in Reno this time tomorrow." He held out a bill of lading, and Dynamite signed it and kept the carbon duplicate. "Moller oughta be here any time. He was right behind me at the river, but the drawbridge got him."

"Good old Commodore," said Dynamite. "That'll make him ornerier'n buckskin. He

46

sure hates not to be first."

"Well, take it easy boys!" said Done Movin' and was on his way.

We stood outside the scales and watched the big diesel pull away into the mist, heard it shift for the slope by the beet-pulp pit, and shift again for the level of the county road, and go away up into the hills till only an echo came back faintly, like the baying of a hound.

"One gone," said Dynamite. "One gone and a dozen to go. We may as well get back to sleep."

He spoke of Moller who would bring in the next truck. They called him Commodore because he told everybody what to do, and they laughed at him because he had no authority. He'd kill himself to get in first, never stopped for a beer and a sandwich, only for fuel. And once in a while, when he telephoned home to get his orders as all drivers did, and the dispatcher gave him orders for the others, too, he had his reward.

We heard another diesel roar, and the sound of heavy gears working on the turn beyond the barn. Commodore was coming.

This time Dynamite left me alone and went away to fix the gates in the alley and balance the scales. In the darkness, my head still burning, I watched Commodore roll up slowly and put the door of his truck even with the chute on the first try — a pretty good piece of work for after midnight. The engine idled down, Commodore got out, and stopped before the headlights to look at his watch, and next moment he stood beside me on the dark strip of footboard that runs along a cattle chute, just the outline of him against the fog.

"Well, you made her," I said.

"Yeah," said Commodore, sympathetic as stone. "Where's Dynamite?"

"Down the line."

"Anyone ahead of me?"

"One," I said.

"Who was it? Henry?"

"A guy named Done Movin'."

"Well, that's Henry, ain't it . . . ? I seen him at the Bridge."

I was trying to get the door open but couldn't because Commodore had done such a good job of pulling up to the chute he had wedged it. "Here," said Commodore, "lemme show ya." He jumped down and wrenched and tore the door away and counted the cattle carefully as they came off, twenty-four head, somehow managing always to keep his back to me, as though maybe I had shown myself a member of some inferior race, unworthy of a clear front view.

Ten minutes later a first draft was on the scales, but still no Commodore appeared. "OK!" yelled Dynamite, and I remembered my job was to count cattle without being killed. Dynamite had said to stand out in front. Dynamite had laughed loudly and long. The misgiving went through me like a sudden pain that Dynamite and Jaydee Jones were one of a kind. "OK, OK!" sang Dynamite, "what's holdin' up the dee-tail?"

I barely put a finger on the latch. The heavy door leaped open and swung back, and somehow there I was alone, just I, squarely in the black mouth of the scales, from where there came a bawling and a seething and a splintering of redwood, as though all hell were in there ready to break loose. But it didn't. Not an animal offered to move. My blood was running better, and I took a step backward. A thin stream of yearlings trickled by. I counted them easily. When the stream became too large, I stepped forward, thinning it. If the yearlings ran too thin, I stepped backward, and their flow increased. There was nothing to it.

"Twenty-four head!" I yelled.

"That's what I got," boomed the voice of Commodore like a grenade exploding in the little shed, yet it was meant for me — a hard kind of compliment. Commodore ex-

49

plained to Dynamite why he had come late: "So when I got back from Phoenix, I told 'em I wasn't ready to go . . . I'd been out a hundred hours then . . . but they said . . . 'Now, listen here, T. S. Ordway wants these cattle, and whose name is wrote bigger around here, his or yours?' That's what the dispatcher said. So I gassed up and hit the road. I was the last one into Havermeyers, last one loaded out. I lent a hand to all the other guys . . . not one of 'em stayed to help me. But I know that Strawberry cut-off, see, where she hits the ridge this side of Nelson's Corner, so I took a left on Eighty-Eight and saved two hours and came in flying clear to the River Bridge, leading *all* the way. And there I had to stop and fuel, and, while the hose was in the tank, I seen Henry's Number Four go by, but I'd have caught him even yet, if the god-dammed draw-bridge hadn't stopped me." As he thought of what this bridge had done, the lines in the face of Commodore grew deeper still, like iron bands cutting into wood. He asked no sympathy; he gave the facts. He was a Prussian, and he punished himself and his machine of rubber, steel, and diesel oil with concrete miles, as he would have punished all flesh and blood until it submitted, or became steel. "If anyone wants me," he said, as he was leaving, "I'll be at the Princess Hotel in Sacramento."

The diesel roared full-throated; the air brakes sighed; Commodore became an echo, fading in the night.

Now trucks came rapidly — two at a time, three, four — and their snoring in the line before the barn, their many-colored twinkling lights and shouts and horns made the yard look like an estuary filled with ships, or a great river anchorage with vessels waiting for the tide. In the darkness men became voices. I swore and kicked and sweated over the dank and stinking beds of trucks with comrades I never saw — Oklahoma Dutch, plain Swedish, Spanish, the lingo of Portugee Bill who owned a pool hall in Tulare and ran a bookie business on the side. These men lived quickly and were gone, yet I had known them better than if I'd seen them face to face all day.

A stubby Irishman named Kelly had a spell of trouble. His cattle would not unload. He tried them in Ulster, in South Orange, in Brooklyn, and the best of Frisco cussing, but they wouldn't move. "God damn," he said, breathless on the rafters that hold the open bed of a truck apart, "come out ye sons-of-bitches, it's Kelly talkin'." And they came.

So the hours were used up. At three

o'clock the wind blew the fog away and let us see the stars men know who work by night — late stars, somehow brighter and better than the ones you see around ten o'clock when most people go to bed. They splattered through the sky from north to south, dusty and brown, like somebody had run there with a bucket and spilled them. They looked down, and they knew who worked and who didn't and who owns the world when everything lies quiet. A truck had just pulled away. Dynamite and I stood still in the alley, and the voice of the wind came rising through the boards and rails, reminding us that man is very small and the Earth by night is very long and lonely.

· We had good luck, when the last three loads came in together, even Blue with the broken shaft; but these drivers, nineteen hours on the road, would not go home. They stood around the headlights of the first big Moreland diesel, bills of lading signed, nothing to hold them but their cigarettes and talk of what had happened in the day: "It was just where the Grapevine hits concrete and makes four lanes, takes off steep there beyond Bakersfield ten mile. So Kelly had her flying high and wide, comin' off in over-drive, you know, with me a-chasin'. Right there was where he blowed 'er. Sure thought he was gone. . . . Took her to the fourth lane and met a tanker coming up, so he took her back, and she hit the ditch with her right three and dug a furry and a cloud of dust you could see by the moon. And his load got shiftin' and the frames picked up the sway and he cut a wiggle like a snake down U.S. Forty-Four. Oh, I tell you, watching him was misery. I sweat cold. I wished the bastard would spill and put me out of pain, but he never . . . the crazy Irishman. I'd have jumped or prayed or done something sensible, but not him . . . not Kelly. He rode her through and brought her out the end a-weavin' in that traffic like a maiden through the daisy chain. . . ."

A deputy dispatcher had come along, red-haired, clean, and young American as football and corduroy trousers. He told the others where to go. "Potts," he said, "you beat it to Eureka. Lay over there. Call in tomorrow, Fresno Operator Thirteen, and she'll tell you where to go. Blue, you get that propeller shaft to the warehouse, and after breakfast . . . that's six o'clock for you, that ain't very long now . . . you take Henley's Number Nine and meet Joe Streets at Appleton, the junction there, and he'll give you his load for the city, and you take 'em right on in. He has to be at Winnemuca this time Monday to haul sheep, and he's been out three days. Charlie, I don't care what the hell you do. You might even go to bed somewheres, but make damn' sure it's alone!"

Minute after minute they lingered, stretching this longest, hardest day until somebody mentioned steak, and the idea grew, and finally it was agreed they should meet at a certain diner at a certain red neon sign where Highway 18 cuts the Danvers Slough. So they got in and gunned their motors till the sleeping yards roared back the sound, and with a shout and a touch of the horn they were gone off homeward in the night. We stood alone and listened for them, shifting on familiar slopes and turns, and heard them baying far along the valley till at last no sound came back.

The job was done.

Day came rapidly, as I crossed the silent quadrangle of garages and heard Dynamite's old Packard labor home. I entered the washroom to clean myself and have a drink — the night's work had dried me out — and there at the sink was Jaydee Jones, washing with a bar of bright red soap.

I put my lips under a faucet and took a drink.

Jaydee rubbed his face hard with his

towel. "B'lieve I've took the pleurisy," he said, rubbing his chest and shoulder vigorously. "Got *such* a pain." And he made circles in the air with his shoulder and right arm. I knew there was nothing in the world the matter with Jaydee, that Jaydee knew this, and knew I knew it. Once burned and twice wary, I washed my hands and said nothing.

"That old bunkhouse," went on Jaydee. "That damned old *thing!* Why, there's a westerly gale acrosst my cot I'd be proud to see Columbus have."

I suggested a compress of hot towels.

"Reckon so?" said Jaydee. "Dunno about hot towels. Had a little cousin Sally to git a lung blistered by a hot towel her mammy give her. . . . Oh, I reckon I *could* heat one just a little. But I kind o' hate to, thinkin' about what it done to Sally Mae. Git yore cattle in?"

"Yeah," I said, "we got 'em. Took us all night but we finally got 'em."

"You stayed with her, eh?" said Jaydee, looking out at me for the first time from under his towel. "W-e-l-l, my old daddy used to tell me what I done by night was worth twice what I could do by day, providin' I weren't caught at it."

Jaydee's dark expression never changed,

55

but he didn't bother to go on rubbing with the towel. I began to wash. When Jaydee saw I had no soap, he said — "Here y'are. Use mine." — and flipped me the bright red bar.

Afterward, I went indoors and sat on the edge of my bed and began unlacing two shoes that suddenly felt made of lead, not leather. I didn't want to sleep. I wanted to go back outside and talk longer with Jaydee; but some cranes that had been roosting in the cypress trees flew away, making harsh cries, and I watched them go across the field, trailing each other through the early light.

I lay down then and fell asleep, knowing, without bothering to care just why, that El Dorado Investment Company had room for me.

# QUICK AND THE CAT

I suppose we all have something of Quick's obsession. Two pistol shots resounded through the cave like thunderclaps, and he had added a pair of mountain-lion kittens to his season's take. He had made a record take that season.

His dogs came pushing past him, eager to be in at the kill. He drove them outside and dragged the kittens along, noting the heaps of bones, of deer, of sheep, of a colt. The old mother lion had piled high the trophies that would make her the great trophy. Flashing his light along the walls, Quick noticed the painting of the Indian god. It had sunk so deeply into the sandstone that, although the surface had been sloughing off for centuries, the grotesque figure, vermilion-red, with the head of a demon and the body of a man, was still visible. It squatted there, arms upraised like a wrestler flexing his muscles, except that where the biceps should have been were additional heads of the same weird configuration as the central one, all unblinking witnesses to what happened in the cave.

Indians were long gone from the Hurricane Deck country, but their mysterious presence remained. Quick stuck his knife blade into the painting to see how deeply the stain penetrated, and after nearly an inch still could not see the end of it. In frustration he slashed the central face, leaving a long, cruel scar. Then he skinned his kill in expert fashion, throwing a carcass to each of his dogs and adding the pelts to the pack where he carried his corn meal, his tin pot, his salt, and his extra flashlight batteries. Then he hit the trail.

It was a warm, clear day for November. He could see nearly a hundred miles across the high country, because Hurricane Deck loomed above its surroundings like a ship above the sea. Its sandstone ledges were the decks; the scattering pines — the masts; the cave openings — cabin doorways; and roundabout in crests and troughs, like the sea, the wilderness stretched. Hurricane Deck was a remote and inaccessible place, used as last resort by Indians, lions, wild cattle. Stockmen or forest rangers might find their way to it in summer, but in winter only Quick went there. The danger of being caught by storms, such as had scalloped the caves and weird, turret-shaped formations, was great.

The mother lion's trail led him down into the headwaters of the Jack Knife on the north and around through Frenchman's Flat and the Pyramid Rocks into the Twilight Country. Quick followed it at a running walk, keeping within earshot of his dogs. On such a fresh trail they gave plenty of sound, and he could hear them whine with eagerness from time to time. The pug marks were enough to make them do that — big around as the palm of your hand, fresh earth spurted at the sides, a mark appropriate to the last of the lions. After her there would be no more. Quick had cleaned out the others, and, if she ran for a week, he would inevitably get her, too.

'Lions did not tree in that country; there were few trees. Through generations of ground travel the cats had developed a gait like a wolf's and abnormally strong legs and lungs that could carry them for days at a time.

Quick went on hands and knees under the chaparral, hand over hand up bluffs, or sliding like an avalanche down a hillside. It was while doing this years before that he had been bitten on the hand by a rattlesnake but had merely slashed the place with his knife and sucked out the poison and after a day's rest gone on, with his hand wrapped in a red bandanna. Quick was tough. When he hunted, he wore two pairs of blue jeans and three hickory-gray shirts for protection against brush. He wore an odd-looking, city man's felt hat. He was something of a character, Quick was. Bound and determined to kill the big cats. He used to say he didn't feel safe so long as one of them was left alive.

At dark, he turned on his flashlight and kept going. Twenty hard miles behind him, he stopped next morning for a bait of corn meal, took time to build a fire by a stream and boil water, and to rest briefly after eating. One thing must have puzzled him about that trail: it led straight, none of the usual windings, as if the cat did not care to try to throw him off.

She moved all day up the east fork of the Desolation. Yet, toward evening, he found the dogs finishing a deer she'd taken time to kill. That decided Quick; he settled down to get her, if he had to walk all winter.

Five days and ninety miles farther along in the wildest, roughest country imaginable he came out again onto the dividing ridge, the backbone of the wilderness that led eventually to Hurricane Deck, and saw she was taking him in a great circle. His food was low. He was tired and so were the dogs. But he felt confident now that he understood her game. He knew the trick of circling for the last stand near home. The end could not be far and the weather had held; the day was warm and still.

On the level going of the ridge among pine and cedar, he gained steadily. By midafternoon the dogs were sounding eager, and the Deck loomed close ahead. The wind, too, had freshened. Since noon it had settled into the northeast, and the sky had grown overcast with thin gray clouds that obscured the sun but did not shut it out entirely.

She led him straight out across the top of the Deck. The voices of the dogs went up a notch as if they would bring her to bay at any minute. Going at a run to be in at the kill, leaping among the broken rocks along the sharp summit of the Deck, Quick slipped as he glanced up to see whether the first snowflakes were only a flurry or the real thing.

He fell in a tumbling, downhill slide until the red branches of a manzanita bush stopped him, and there he stayed, pressing his head into the ground to hold back the pain from his broken leg, while the loose rock rolled on past, and the snow swept over him.

He could not see beyond a few feet, and,

as he lay there helpless, he could hear the dogs going farther and farther away. He whistled. He shouted. But nothing came except the snow, thick and fast, covering him as he lay.

He would have to find shelter or freeze. Groping around to see if he had all his equipment, his hand came upon the empty pistol holster. He had fallen only about twenty feet, but they might as well have been a thousand. To climb back up the hill and look for a gun was impossible. He groped everywhere within reach. Then he began to drag himself down toward the ledges and caves that gave the Deck its name. He hoped the dogs would let the lion go, in the storm, and come looking for him before the snow erased his trail.

It is possible he did not recognize the place at first because of the way the snow altered the landscape; then he flashed his light on the wall and saw the painting of the Indian god. He began to wonder then. A few more minutes, exposed to the storm, would have finished him. He dragged himself inside over the heaps of bones to the very back of the cave where it was warm and dry. True, there was a stench of death and an atmosphere weird as the other world itself — what with the god of the vanished Indians on the wall, its head defaced, the bloodstains of the kittens in the crumbled stone of the floor and the dung, very old and brittle, of wild cattle that had once used the place as refuge. The dung gave Quick an idea. He reached into the pocket of his inner shirt and found the matches there still dry. He began collecting the dung. Then he made a fire near the back wall of the cave, but with a space between large enough for him to sit propped up. He used his pack as cushion — the kitten pelts made it a soft one — and settled himself to wait for the dogs. With his remaining corn meal, dog meat, too, if necessary, and with snow water to drink, he could exist for many days, until help came or his leg healed. The fire gave him encouragement, and there was plenty of fuel.

He watched the snow falling across the cave's mouth, like a distant curtain blown by the wind, but he could not hear the wind. He could hear nothing in the depths of his cave and could see only its irregular opening, about as high as a man, where the snow turned gradually from white to gray as twilight came. He thought of the dogs. He whistled once or twice, but it accomplished nothing except to start tiny avalanches crumbling from the sandstone walls. The place was so constructed by Nature that a sharp sound did that. Still, he wondered where the dogs were. Then the thought occurred to him, with a shudder, that she might have killed them.

Just at dark he saw the firelight reflected from a pair of eyes at the mouth of the cave. It was the sight he'd been dreading. Then he let out a shriek. The eyes did not move.

He grabbed a bone and threw it, but he had been so weakened that the bone fell short by many feet. He shouted again and tried to focus his flashlight on the eyes, but the fire got in the way. Near fainting, he fell back against the wall. He had his knife. He took it out and opened the big blade and laid it beside him, but kept the long, club-like flashlight in his hand. He watched all night, and at dawn the eyes disappeared.

The snow continued to fall. He watched it hour after hour, longing to get some to quench his thirst. Thirst was killing him. And nothing stirred at the cave mouth. Quick began dragging himself toward the snow. It was slow and painful work, making his way across the litter of bones and refuse, but finally he got to the mouth of the cave and was about to scoop himself a handful of snow when a snarl warned him. He could not see her, but she was right there, around the corner of rock.

He dragged himself back in a panic to where he had been. The effort and fright nearly made him lose consciousness, but he forced himself to stay alert, propped against the cave wall, putting bits of dung on the fire from time to time. After a while his thirst grew less and finally disappeared, as if his fever had consumed it, and he did not feel anything very keenly any more. He was not much alarmed when at evening she came inside the cave.

She was a white lion. The snow had caked all over her, making her loom twice as large and strange, but there was nothing hostile about her. She might have been any animal coming in out of the weather. He felt relieved now that he could see her. She took a step or two inquiringly toward him, then stopped and watched, her tail switching back and forth every few seconds.

He made a sudden move as an experiment. She did not flinch. He gave a shout that was only a croak, and the piece of burning dung he tried to throw at her fell from his fingers. Then he lay back, in his weakness, and watched her. She had not moved. The snow began to melt from her and run onto the floor. She walked aside to a dry place and lay down. Quick felt almost reassured to have her company, with the storm whirling outside. She was so self-possessed. It seemed to soothe him. They faced each other silently hour after hour until she merged into the fantasies of his delirium.

Once it seemed that the three faces of the Indian painting were alive and watching him. He tried to evade their glance by shutting his eyes, but when he opened them, the faces were still watching. The one he had scarred seemed to gaze at him most relentlessly.

He woke to find the lion very close, barely out of reach beyond the fire, and the fire nearly dead. He could see each individual, bristling whisker, like those of a catfish, and the intent, expressionless yellow eyes with their dark cat's slits in the center. He jerked upright with a shout that made her lift her head and look at him, as a dog lying by a hearth lifts its head at some sudden noise and looks. Then she put her head back down on her paws and continued to watch him, like a dog. He could see her breathe. He thought of his dead dogs. He heaped dung on the fire. The blaze made her retire a few feet, and there she lay down again.

Once during the day that followed she went to the mouth of the cave and ate snow, but when Quick tried to do likewise, she warned him back with a snarl. Then he began to laugh. He laughed and laughed deliriously and was soon raving at the lion. He told her she represented every brute thing hateful to mankind. He said as long as she was alive he could not sleep and that was why he had determined to kill her. She listened, unperturbed. When he saw that nothing he could say had any effect on her, he took the kittens' skins out of the pack and flaunted them at her. "You may have got me!" he cried in a feeble squeak. "But I've got you. Right here! After you, there *can't* be any more!" In his frenzy he forgot to put dung on the fire.

The only witness to what happened then was the Indian god.

We found that the bones had not been dismembered as is usually the case with a lion kill. However, she had managed to spirit away every article of his clothing and equipment, as if wanting nothing to detract from what remained. Each bone had been mouthed lovingly and was polished bright and clean, and there he lay, preëminent among all trophies in that gruesome collection, a human skeleton.

# DYNAMITE'S DAY OFF

Dynamite had asked for Sunday off to go to the rodeo at Sacramento and had been refused, and his wrath was greater than Achilles's. He had entered the bronc' riding and steer decorating and hoped, for one afternoon, to forget he was married to a wife and four children and worked for three dollars a day, seven days a week, in a feed yard full of silly, fat cattle. Instead, he and I drove two cars of steers to the station, and I saw a spark kindling in his eyes that threatened to explode all twenty-six years of his Utah brimstone and powder.

We put the steers in the loading corrals and got ready the first of two empty cattle cars that stood on the siding. Its door stuck, as car doors always do; and Dynamite, in wrenching at it, crushed his hand against the side of the car and drew it out bleeding, with an oath. The bit of animal yellow in his blue eyes widened. He unfastened the bullboard and dropped the wooden apron, and I pulled forward the sliding wings of the chute. We walked down the cleated ramp to where the steers stood in the crowding pen, staring at us like great fat dogs. We wanted twenty-seven in each car — one for Los Angeles, one for Denver. Dynamite counted them as they passed. We crammed the twenty-seven in the car with terrible shouts. We climbed over the gray-bleached fence and cut loose the car. I took the Johnson bar, which is a kind of pry that fits under the wheels and will move a train if your back is strong enough, and Dynamite pushed, and we got her rolling.

When the second car was in place and ready to load, we went down into the crowding pen, and I counted the steers. There were twenty-eight.

I said to Dynamite: "They're only twenty-six steers in that first car."

He ran up quickly — he hadn't yet said a word to me — and counted my cattle again through the slats of the car. There were twenty-eight. Then he began to swear. Once in a small California town I saw a Filipino run amuck and come screaming down Main Street, flailing with a chain at everything in his way. That was how Dynamite sounded. His voice rose into a wail, singsong, like a maniac's. "God damn . . . god damn . . . *god* damn . . . !" He swung ape-fashion inside the car, hanging from the overhead beam, and kicked a big red steer in

70

the face until its nose bled and it backed out into the ramp. I dropped the bull-board and held the rest.

We got the Johnson bar again and went to work; and by the time we had the first car back in place, we felt as though we had moved the whole Southern Pacific.

Then Dynamite went for the steer. Now, when an animal has once been loaded and come out, to get him back again is like getting a convict back to jail. Dynamite and that steer went around and around. The steer got mad. Dynamite got madder. The steer ran him up the fence. Dynamite got a post and hit the steer over the head till one eye was shut and the blood ran from its nose, and he kept on till the animal gave a shake of its head and a bloody snort and ran up into the car.

"Well," I said, "it's a good thing they don't eat the head."

"The son-of-a-bitch," said Dynamite.

Our horses were tied at the far end of the corrals. As we got on, I saw a black pickup truck drive alongside our cars of cattle and stop.

"There's the boss come to give you hell," I said.

We rode the horses through a side gate and around toward the tracks. I saw somebody that wasn't the boss at all get out of the pickup, standing on one leg, and draw a crutch after him.

"It's that old man," said Dynamite, not to me, but to the earth in general, as you would say a profane thing. From him this was profanity. He and old Reuben Child were great friends. Dynamite could admire any man who was a Texan and who, besides, had been a champion roper and rider. Rube lived now in a house the Company had given him, and like an old hunting dog never failed to know when cattle were on the move and hurry down in his pickup to be there.

He waved the crutch at us and took a shovel from the bed of the truck with his other hand. He had backed his pickup to the low ridge of sand that collects along the tracks in front of the chute — bedding from the cars, kicked out by the cattle.

I got off and tied my pony and said: "Hey now, old man, stealing our sand?"

"Oh, no," said Rube, "the Company told me I could have it." And his face lit up as though they had given him a new house.

"You'd better hand me that shovel," I said.

I thought Dynamite had ridden on. I knew he was ready for one of his evenings at the village saloon with Pete, the bartender, the trustee of our misfortunes. I rather wished he had gone on, but he couldn't — he couldn't quite pass up old Rube. He got off sulkily and came to us.

"Hello, Dynamite," said Rube, raising his Texan's drawl till he sounded like a little girl.

"Hi, Rube," said Dynamite.

"Come on," I said, "there's another shovel in the truck. Get busy."

In five minutes we had the pickup loaded.

"That's enough, fellers," said Rube. "I only want it for the dooryard. Here . . . ," he said, reaching into the compartment of the front seat, "here, this is Sunday. Have a drink on it."

"Naw," said Dynamite, "I gotta go."

"Have a drink," said Rube.

"I gotta be going." Dynamite untied his brown nag from the fence.

"Come on, have a drink," said Rube and held out the bottle.

Dynamite took it, holding the tie-rope with his other hand, and tilted down a good long shot. "That whiskey's all right," he said.

The bottle went around, and Rube gave it back to Dynamite for another shot. "Say," said Rube, "isn't that saddle a Harney Lee?"

"Yeah," Dynamite said, "one the Evans Company named after him."

. The saddle was older than Dynamite himself. The cover had peeled from the high flat horn and worn clear away from places on the stirrup leathers, so that you could see the latigo straps; its skirt had shriveled like the skin of a drying fruit, but in the center of the tree, where a man did his riding, the leather had the color of dark mahogany shining in the sun — a deep red quality — and here was all the life of the saddle.

The wind blew the mane of the brown nag and made him put his ears up, so that he and the saddle were a picture for a book.

Dynamite looked at them proudly. "That's a hell of a fine saddle, Rube," he said.

Rube sat down on the running board of the car, facing west, with the sun full on him, took a sack of Bull Durham from his pocket, and began to roll a cigarette. The wind bent the brim of his cattleman's hat and slapped him in the face, but he pushed the hat back with one hand and went on rolling the tobacco in his other, and never lost a grain.

"Shore is a country to blow," he said.

Rube was a veteran of the range. His face, drawn by years of pain from the broken hip, had on it the indelible stain of Western sun. His large, clear eyes seemed always to be searching some horizon; his ears were classic American, protruding just a little; and there was about him a peculiar decency and patience. When he smiled, his face shone almost in a heavenly way, as Lincoln's did.

"You fellers ever hear the story of Harney Lee?"

"I never did," said Dynamite.

Rube held the cigarette up to his mouth and licked the end of it affectionately. We knelt beside him, close to the track, and the cattle in the car above us stomped around and kicked out little puffs of sand through the slats of the car.

Rube smiled. "Makes me laugh to see cattle nowadays. Gracious, they ain't cattle . . . they's responsibility. Gotta be fed this, gotta be fed that, gotta be fed this very time o' day. Why, where would them great outfits of old time have been . . . Turkey Track and Circle Dot . . . if they'd had to go out every day at half-past two and *feed* their cattle? Those fellers depended on their cattle, not their cattle on them. And by cattle I mean longhorns. It was them built the West and don't you never forget it." Rube stuck the cigarette in his mouth, but it was not right, and he spat it out and threw it away. "My story is about the time when cattle still had horns . . . about the greatest rider that ever rode and the wind that made him great and the horse that killed him.

"In the fall of 'Ninety-Eight we was coming from Chihuahua toward the Río Grande and, fellers, that's a long country . . . long and dry . . . and, when ye've been out sixteen weeks, she's uphill all the way. We counted two hundred horses and six thousand longhorn steers. Red Handle was our boss . . . finest ever that trailed a herd . . . and his top rider was Harney Lee. I think there was thirty-three of us, all told. Men was cheap in them days . . . it was cattle cost the money."

Dynamite interrupted: "This here Harney Lee . . . what did he look like?"

"Oh, he was a Texas man," said Rube. "Looked like a giant but he weren't so big. Had a mustache . . . eyes that got narrer at the outside. You can see his picture in books. . . . We'd been out all summer with the wagon and was headed home with what we'd done, six thousand old mosshorns from 'way back that till we come along had never seen a horse from the day they was born. Some had the Hourglass and Horse-shoe brands. Some was mavericks, virgin

76

pure. What I mean . . . they was cattle! You got up on a high place and give a squall or two, and all over the county puffs of dust went up, and that meant cattle heading for the next state. But we rode with 'em step for step, and by the time we started for the Río Grande, they knowed a cowboy.

"One afternoon I seen 'em acting queer. Five or six would stop together and raise their heads and sniff and stand a while . . . and in a herd the better part of four mile long this slows you up considerable. Well, I was a youngster then, and, when I got in for supper, I asked Red Handle what was the matter . . . he was eatin' beans . . . never eat nothing but beans, old Red, but he sure was a boss. He could water six thousand head in a hole the size of this room and never get it muddy. 'Dust,' he says. 'They smell a dust somewheres . . .' and went on eatin' his beans.

"Well, that put a wiggle in my spine, but I never said so. I noticed the wind had come up a little, and, when the cocktail riders got in and the nighthawkers was ready to start, I saw Red go over and talk a while to 'em. There begun to be something in the air. Cookie gathered in his washing and his pots and pans, like he'd seen the enemy already. At daylight we was on the move. We kept the trail three hours, but that daylight never growed. Then we knew it was dust. By noon she'd rose up there in the north big and blue, like night had got around that way and was coming down on us . . . and, when she got closer, she turned red around the edges, as if fire was in her, and then yellow. We went slower and slower. By now, them steers would stop every few feet and snort and sniff the air, and, when two-o'clock come, they wasn't moving at all. We'd had 'em to water at a dry lake on a piece of country flat as your hand, and it was plain they'd go no farther. Pretty quick them as had laid down got up. It become terrible dark. Then altogether them cattle begun to move . . . *south*. They was like water after a rain, altogether, a-walkin' just as steady, and, when the first grains of sand hit 'em, they begun to trot, all six thousand. Then we rode.

"Ever been in dust? Well, when you have, don't never worry no more 'bout going to hell 'cause you've been there already. In a duster you burn just as slow. It's like the devil come at you first with sandpaper, then with fire, and . . . oh, mercy me . . . how he does hurt! Seems he's gonna skin the clothes right off you and eat out your eyes and nose and ears like fire eats out a holler tree. You see him hit them mesquite bushes . . . big, spiny fellers thirty feet across . . . and shrink 'em till they're no bigger'n a porcupine. Behind every bush and rock he makes an eddy, as does a running stream, but don't git in there or you *will* choke, 'cause there the sand boils right straight up. You'll smell the stink o' creosote bushes being broke and chewed up. You'll see chuckwallas, and such, run under foot till you think your pony'll trip hisself . . . they can't find no hole the dust don't smoke 'em out of. And maybe you'll look around all of a sudden and find cattle on both sides, and then you won't know what to do, so you drift with 'em. Don't never try to head a herd. It can't be done. Sometimes you can bend 'em, but head 'em . . . never. If you meet a rider, you think it's Billy the Kid out to rob a stage . . . face in a bandanna, hat tied hard and fast, but some way the rheumatics has took him, and he's bunched like an ape in the saddle. One feller I saw lose his hat, and that's just barin' your head for the execution. What I mean . . . it's a serious thing. He had a gunny sack tied behind his saddle, but before he could get to it, I seen a blush start up his face that meant the skin was going."

Rube continued gravely: "Once I looked

around and *did* see only cattle on both sides, and there was nothing I could do. I thought left was out and bore that way, edging mighty easy through them horns, and finally I run clear of cattle and found two other fellers and knowed then that I had the flank. We drifted quite a while, shaping the herd the best we could, feeling them steers more'n we saw 'em, and after a long time Harney Lee come up behind us with five men. He'd been clear around the tail of that herd. Red Handle'd sent him with half the riders they could find and kept the other half, and now we was organized. Six of us strung along the flank, and three went up with Harney on the point. He rode a little Steeldust horse, I remember . . . one of them Texas ponies just the color of dust, and it was hard to follow him. We stayed all day, bending the cattle as we could, and that wasn't much, 'cause cattle traveling that way don't have much give in 'em. Pretty quick it got dark. This here was night, gen-u-ine. Once the dust blew clean away over us like a rainstorm does, and we could see a piece of the moon up there, brown and rotten as an apple. Then the dust come on again, and all night it kept after us and all next day, and it seemed we was a-goin' backward where we'd been last summer . . .

I mean the year itself was goin' back. We'd pass a gully or a rock we knowed, and they'd rise up there to say we'd wasted our time and never would get home.

"That day four more fellers joined us, but we didn't eat and seen no sign of the remuda. I never cared. I had my best horse under me . . . a buckskin bronc' named Anesthetic, and what I mean . . . he'd put many a man to sleep. But when that kind tries you and sees you don't fade, they become good horsy. For a tough ride give me a buckskin every time . . . they can't be beat.

"Well, the second day got on . . . we couldn't tell the time . . . it all run together and become evening. And now the steers was dryin' up and gettin' mad . . . sal-*i*-ver hung outer their mouths like spiders was inside a-spinnin' threads, and you had to be chary 'bout getting close, or them big leaders would turn and root you one. But they kept right on . . . they was walkin' mad.

"Harney would look 'em over and ride up and down the line. We got to calling him General and saluted as he come, and other things men does when they're very tired. He was so all-over dust you couldn't tell who it was coming, 'cept by how he set his horse, always for'rd thataway in the saddle, ready to make his ride. He'd laugh at us, blowing dust off his mustache, and call us chuck-walla sons-of-bitches. He told me one thing . . . to keep my Forty-Five inside my pants or the sand would ruin it. He packed two guns hisself. I could see 'em bulge under his chaps, and he rode a low-lyin', double-rigged saddle with the short cantle and high horn . . . one they named after him. Oh, he was a giant of a man, Harney Lee, but to look at he weren't so big. . . .

"Now after quite a spell . . . might have been noon, might have been three-o'clock . . . he comes to me and says . . . 'Young Rube, we're a-gonna bend this herd. I want you to ride and tell Red Handle I need men.' Reckon my face showed what I felt . . . that bending the herd would be as easy as bending the storm . . . 'cause he so-bered clear up and says . . . 'We got a alkali lake ahead of us, and the water's poison . . . we can't let the cattle to it.' Well, then I rode. I got lost. I dried clear out. I couldn't find the end of the herd. Once I passed an *ocotillo*, a cactus that's all joints and fingers, and that's the only time I ever wanted to be a cactus, 'cause them *ocotillos* can breathe through their stems. Then I found Red, and he looked awful poor . . . he'd had a fall and sprained his arm. He took eight fellers and told 'em what Harney wanted and all he said

82

was . . . 'All right, boys. I want to hear ye've made this ride.'

"I led the way back, and, when we come again upon the left flank, the sky got terrible dark, and then all of a sudden she lighted up, and there was the greatest sight on which *my* eyes ever laid. There was Harney Lee and seven men goin' alone ag'in' the point, *and they had her bent!* Seven of 'em had her bent. They rode her down out of a per-pet-tual circle, riding close together, single file, with not enough room between for cattle to come through, and always the tightest part of that circle was ag'in' the herd, and here the guns was flashing, and the boys would make their ride . . . pressing in and in . . . and now a big steer would take to 'em and run 'em out of line, and they'd shy off and come 'round the loop and hit the herd again . . . and always Harney led 'em, pouring fire in the air from both his guns. We hurried and joined up with 'em and made a bigger, heavier circle, with never room between us for a steer to pass . . . and we bent them critters clear around.

"Them as was fightin' mad and wouldn't bend we shot, and the rest kept on . . . but always to the right, just a little to the right. We hit a kind of watercourse that in such country was like a line on the palm of your hand, but it helped . . . and here we done what no men ever done . . . we milled that herd. Yep, milled her. Red shaped her from the other side, but Harney Lee it was that milled her, tucked her in till she was running like a rattler on her own tail. Time and time again he led us in, flyin' in the twilight like a man who rode the wind. Slowly she wound up and run down, and some critters at the inside fell and was chewed like meat in a grinder . . . and then just as we thought we had 'er, the whole thing come undone, snapped open like a willer branch that's been rolled up, and away went them critters down the plain. Three times we rolled 'em up and three times they come undone, but on the fourth they stayed. . . .

"We held the herd all night, and next morning the day broke clear, and we eased 'em up this wash into a new country. By noon we'd found water, running water, and made camp. Toward evening here come Cookie and the remuda, two hundred ponies. They'd drifted with the storm the same as we. The wranglers said they'd gone ahead and the herd had followed em' like ponies will a man in the dark . . . in a way, that's the rest of my story, but anyhow . . . from this stream of running water Red got the idea for going home along the Coche

Hills where there was more streams like it and a storm couldn't git right to us, if it come again. We laid over a couple of days, and within three more we'd hit a rimrock country with cañons and some timber.

"We all stood turns nighthawking the ponies, three of us, usually, 'cause there was Mexicans around, and this far from home we couldn't take no chances. There's nobody loves good horseflesh as does a Mexican.

"This particular night Harney Lee was on the graveyard shift, him and a couple of fellers . . . one called Sleepy Head and another silly kind of feller called Jack. The herd was on a slope above a cañon, and, when the next shift come, it got to Jack first. He'd seen old Sleepy, dozin' over there, and had an *i*-dee for some fun. He gives his horse to the others to hold and slips over there right easy with his quirt behind old Sleepy.

"You know how horses are at night, up and down three or four times, and so long as some are up and feedin', the rest won't scare, but this particular night it happened all the herd was asleep, and, when Jack smacked old Sleepy's nag across the rump, he jumped twenty feet down hill and bucked old Sleepy off and broke in two and went down through that herd just a-buckin' and a-raisin' hell . . . and them ponies was to their feet like one horse and away down the cañon. Well, square in their way was Harney Lee. You boys never seen horses comin' at you wild in the dark, but it's a terrible thing. They'll run you down the same as steers and twice as quick. Their shoes knockin' the stones sends out all manner of sparks . . . red and yeller and blue. Harney seen it comin' and could have got away, but instead he turned his pony and begun to ride . . . same little Texas pony he'd rode through all the dust. He knowed how horses will foller a man by night, if you give 'em just the right amount of room, and he figured to wind 'em up somewheres and lead 'em home. And that's what he did. We found the herd next day up again the rimrock, and in the cañon by the trail lay Harney where he'd fell . . . a badger'd dug his hole right there." Old Rube stopped talking. The cold spring wind slapped through our clothes and made the wiry grasses sing in the ditch beside the track. "Pity . . . ," said Rube. "Pity he couldn't have died upon his greatest day . . . but all of us can't do that . . . we gotta die in beds or, if we're lucky, just-a-doin' our job like Harney done."

Dynamite gave a wet sniff and tried to hide it in a sneeze, wiping his mouth with his shirt sleeve. There was a single poppy growing in the track between two ties, and he plucked it and mashed the petals through his fingers.

"Well, by God, Rube," he said, "that was a good story."

# WOMEN AND DYNAMITE

Every winter day at one o'clock Dynamite and I took heavy six-tined forks that were meant to shovel feed for cattle and cleaned the barn, leaving our horses saddled in their stalls, ready for the afternoon round. This was a day that sometimes in a California winter blows like a blessing from the sea. Dynamite that very morning had put on long underwear, expecting a cold snap, and, as he warmed up a little at the end of the fork and began to sweat, the wool tickled his skin and made him itch and swear and blame his wife.

"Woman is a weak-minded outfit, anyway," he said, boosting a load out the window to the compost pile and grinning his little boy's grin. For a lad of twenty-six with a wife and four children, Dynamite had a lot to say. "Never did use undy-wear," he said, "till I got married, nor socks neither. Back home when it come cold we put old newspaper down our boots . . . they's all a man needs till he gets a woman."

Home for Dynamite was any place he happened to be. Once it had been the Utah border, once the Oregon cattle country. . . .

We worked in shadow. Sea wind blowing in the open door swept dust over us from the gray dirt floor of the barn. Outside, trucks were passing on the road; we could see the backs of cattle in their pens beyond, and then the deep adobe fields, tinged by early rains with a faint green shadow of new grass. Far away the Napa Hills rose up and made a line across the open door just even with the stirrup of the boss's saddle, hanging on its peg.

"All right," I heard Dynamite mutter, "here he is."

Jacks, the foreman, stood in the lighted square of doorway — or rather the outline of him; you couldn't see his face, only the light that ran forward along the brim of his hat and in the folds of his overall pants. The Napa Hills cut across him waist high.

He stuck a hand in each hip pocket, rocked a minute on his heels, and told us there was a bulling steer in Pen 81 that ought to come out. Then he went away.

We forked out several loads.

"Notice Jacks there?" said Dynamite, and I could tell he had something on his mind. "Looked pretty big, didn't he?"

I said I guessed he had. But he *had* looked big; I remembered how the Napa Hills came only to his waist.

"He ain't that big, though," said Dynamite, "it was just the light made him look thataway."

I agreed.

"And did ye ever notice him there . . . till he talks he's awful good. He's maybe coming to say you got a raise, or to give ye the day off. You can't tell."

Dynamite with an idea was like a chicken with a seed, taking it up, dropping it, clucking over it several times, and finally either swallowing it or walking away. But if he ever took a thing, it went all the way down; and then the words came tumbling out and spread away over the plain, like his own Colorado River.

Now all this sounded like a big seed, so I waited, and in a minute he said: "See this barn?" He was standing at the window, leaning on his fork, looking out across the compost pile. I came along and pitched a load and said, yes, I did see the barn.

"Sure pretty, ain't it?" said Dynamite.

Well, it did look pretty. It stood off there half a mile away across a grassy field that was so thin and green it looked like water, and the wind ran on it sparkling. The barn was part in shadow, part in sun; and somebody had cut three black squares out of its side that were windows, like ours, and on a hill beyond there was a mist as in the spring.

"Yes, sir," said Dynamite, "that's a fine idee of what a barn should be. Makes you want to git up and start over there, don't it? . . . thinkin' there is all that makes a good barn . . . sweet hay and horses in their stalls, pussycats, saddles, old harness hangin', smellin' like last summer. You say . . . 'By God, that must be the best barn in all the world.' But it ain't, is it?"

"I don't know," I said, "maybe it is."

"Till you get there anyway, it is," said Dynamite, and then he said no more, and I didn't hurry him.

We took our ponies and started on the afternoon round, going first to get the bulling steer and putting him in the hospital. That brought us out on Mill Alley between the pens of cattle, on a knoll above the mill where the wind of forty miles strikes bare and always blows. It took the feed grains from the mangers and stuck them in our eyes and slopped them through our clothes and curled the dust away on a long banner from the ventilator on top of the mill.

Dynamite pulled up his pony. "Hear it?" he said.

"Hear what?" I said.

"That's what it is," said Dynamite. "Damn me, if it ain't!"

He held his hat on with one hand, looking right up at the sky where some power lines crossed, going to the mill. "Don'tcha *hear* it?" he asked.

I said: "What the devil are you talking about?"

"The wind in the wires," said Dynamite.

"What about it?" I said.

"Nothing," said Dynamite. "Nothing about *it*, but about me, plenty . . . 'cause that's the sound I heard the night of the Twentieth September Nineteen Thirty-Three, when I rode off the top o' the world to have a drink and see my girl."

We went on down the knoll and around the hay field to the big stack, where the wind couldn't find us, nor the boss, and there Dynamite told me his story.

"Every year in May we took cattle on the mountain . . . earlier sometimes, if the year was good . . . and always we was champing to get away. Winter in town leaves a feller in the red. Bills here, argy-ments here, some little maiden a-wanting to git married . . . they's no profit. You go along with your feet fixed one way and your mind another, and, if ye get as far as March without meeting the sheriff on the way, you're lucky. March . . . she's better than a drink of whiskey! Then your ponies' hair begins to slip, you're getting out the pack saddles, a-oiling up old leather, and every guy is friendly again for the first time since Christmas.

"We hit the Mormon trail that comes in out o' the desert and takes up past town onto the mountain. Our range was all that as was east of west and north of south, and any more we needed. That country's not like this . . . we don't prison our cattle. The rimrocks is our fences.

"Well, when you first go up, she's hunky-dory. The cattle wants to go, the ponies wants to go . . . they's sick of valley living. All you're cravin' is that feel of hair between your knees and a chance to run and bust him out. You look the other way just a-hoping that pa'tic'lar red steer with the Roman nose and the droop-horn will take a break, 'cause you see he's got a run in him, and sure enough he does, and then you make old mountain smoke.

"My job was what they call the Tennessee Pass, where cattle drifts in summer when the meadow feed goes short, and sometimes they travels all of Eighty Mile Hill clear down to the river, unless I catch 'em first, which I usually does.

"I made lone camp on Aspen Crick, by a big old boulder where there was a cedar tree and a ice cold spring run out of the stone. I made me seats and tables, a corral built of them hairy cedar logs . . . a bed of boughs . . . a canvas lean-to for when it rained. I packed in grain for my pony. I had horseshoes, nails, and pounds and pounds of sowbelly, spuds, and beans . . . and I had all my thoughts of what'd been since last I camped on Aspen Crick. To think 'em I had company. Off south was the Old Man, twelve thousand feet and white with snow all summer long. I could see him there on moonlight nights, hanging off above me like a ghost. I'd sit by the fire then, eating my beans, pounding me some jerky for a stew, and, when I had eat, I'd go on sitting there just to listen — me all alone, you know, and old pony over there in his corral a-munchin'. I'd watch the firelight run up and down a grove of quakies . . . quaking aspens . . . that growed beside the water, thin and white, you know, with del-y-cate leaves like they was people's hair. I'd imagine they *was* people. It was so awful quiet there, seemed like I had a chance to think for the first time . . . and them little trees put me in mind of fellers I knowed. When you was a kid, did you ever sit and think who was your best friends? Well, that's what I done. I'm not ashamed to own it. I wasn't no more'n seventeen, anyways . . . so I thought of Hap, my pard, who'd been with me through many a scrape and was keepin' my other horse, a little sorrel with cat hips. I thought a lot about that cat-hipped sorrel. I needed him to spell old Tony off, and hoped that Hap would take a notion to ride up and see me. Then I thought of Kitty McWilliams and Hoopaloo, both good guys, and of a feller named Harry I met that winter. Handsome Harry, they called him, and he was drunk . . . drunk all the time. Once he was a-gonna meet us at a certain place but never showed, and they found him two days later on the Della Road, froze stiff, drunk. Cedar Bill, I thought about, and others, but amongst them aspen trees was one smaller than the rest, with branches like the arms of ferns, and leaves the wind whispered through and made to dance in the firelight, and that one was my girl, Maxine."

Dynamite put a straw into his mouth and seemed to think of something off the path of his story.

"But that's all right," he said, "thas all right. I had a good time there three months, and then I began to tire. You get so used to yourself. Everything's right where you left it. In the morning you go out and at evening

95

you come back, and, if a squirrel has walked across the table and kicked at the crumbs, you'd know it. And I got tired of hearing nobody's voice but my own, and tired of working with horseflesh and cowflesh and rope and leather, and tired as hell of eatin' alone. I wanted to mix with humankind.

"And so it was this night . . . I'd been out late. There was a change in the weather coming. I could see the sun go down orange out here in Californy, and I guessed that might mean trouble for cowboys. This was late September, see, and by then anything can happen. If snow comes, cattle drift, and you drift with 'em, whether it's a mile or eighty. So I'd made a long round and come out just at evening on the Indian Rock. I could see all the valley, all the desert, all the mountain. Oh, she was a panoramic! Old Tony and I set there and watched her, while down in the valley the lights come on one by one, like little stars. A cluster of 'em made the town. One I knowed was the café my girl Maxine worked, and I wanted to be there awful bad. Now that town didn't amount to *nuthin'!* Why, at high noon it wouldn't make a shadow, and dry, O Jesus! No water run by that place! I don't know why I wanted to go. I'd lived there all my life, but I had to go.

"I says to Tony . . . 'How do you feel?' . . .

and he says . . . 'Fine.' So we piles over the edge.

"I knowed I could make it in three hours, going straight down, and be there before them little stars went out. I'd go right to the café and see Maxine. I'd find Hap and get my sorrel horse, and I'd do a lot of things that would be worth telling later.

"Did ye ever start to go anywheres at night? The how nor why of it don't matter, ye just go. Well, that was the way with me, and I begun to sing, because I was a silly kid then. I sung that song . . . you've heard me.

**_Up_-on my pony,**
**_Up_-on old Tony,**
**To ride o'er the prairie**
**To see my charming Mary. . . .**

"And so I slid off that mountain, and I bet I was something to hear. That country's funny built. She's made of sandstone and looks like somebody threw her up on edge, like a deck of cards. Just when I was flyin' high, one of them cards slipped out from under old Tony, and to me it felt like the whole deck. We just quit the ground and flew a ways, and, when we come down, I was pinned ag'in' a cedar tree, under the saddle, with old Tony waving his feet at the moon and me a-spittin' sandstone and trying to git a-hold of his head. See, I had one leg under the saddle and ag'in' the tree, and, every time he'd move, I'd think that leg was goin' with him.

"We man-o-veered 'round a bit, and I got my short tug on the offside undone, and the saddle slid ahead and let me go. Well, that was all right. My leg was still there, and pretty quick we was on our way down the mountain. I was feeling no pain . . . I couldn't do wrong. Did ye ever feel that way? . . . go through a narrer escape and come out knowing the angels was on your side and you couldn't miss from there on in? I went down that mountain, under them big pines, and I was light enough to fly. I was a-gonna see my girl . . . I was a-gonna have a drink and put my feet under a table and have people bring me things. And I didn't care how long it took, 'cause I had music in me and could have rid to the end of the world.

"The old night opened up and let me down like water does a stone. Air rushin' in my ears was all I heard. I'd watch them little lights go flicker through the trees. They'd been at my feet to start, but now they was pushing away into the desert, and I spurred old Tony to catch 'em. I got thinking of

Maxine at the café. She'd be off at nine. By then my leg would be all swole up and sore, and maybe she'd take me home and rub liniment on it. I'd have a bath first. I knowed a place I could git one for thirty-five cents. They give you medicated soap, too. And then I thought of Hap, my pal, and where I could find him. Probably the Hearty Laugh Saloon . . . and that made me think of the steaks old Jippy served there, and I got hungry as hell. I figured to go there first and have a drink or two and a steak and get the lay of things.

"Just about then I run onto cattle bedded deep in sarvis brush . . . first one scared me, an old cow critter. I thought she was a bear, starting up there in the dark with a stomp and snoof, but I was through the rest afore they could get out of bed, and by the faint light of the moon I knowed they was outlaws. I could see their white horns rise up around me all in a second, like them yucca flowers blooms on the desert.

"Once I come out onto a bench and over a dry meadow, and looked back and saw my dust a-risin' like smoke off'n that black mountain side. Then I run out of the timber into scrub cedars. A cloud come and covered the moon, so I couldn't see only the big things, and run old Tony right over them

99

little trees and got my face slapped bad. Did you ever git a scrape from pine or cedar . . . oily trees? It's like somebody cut you open and poured in fire. But after a while we was down onto the desert, where there's nothing grows but lizards and shad scale, and there I could break old Tony into a lope. It was a mile to the crick bed, and I knowed that farms begun on the other side, and fences. I never reckoned on anything till I got there. But some son-of-a-bitch had run a drift fence right across that desert, and Tony hit 'er at the end of his stride. It was like jumping in a net. I mounted the horn but grabbed leather with both fists and come down. Another horse but Tony would have cut himself in half, and, if folks in that country built fences like they does out here, I guess even he'd o' done it, but this guy, this fence-builder . . . I'd say he come from Californy 'cept he didn't know how to build a fence . . . had just gone out there and put cedar posts in the desert about every hundred yards and hung some wire on 'em. I bet that wire had a give of ten yards. I could get enough slack to twist and break it with my hands. Then I lit a match to have a look at Tony and seen he was cut pretty bad on the chest, poor bastard. He wasn't in very good shape anyway after all summer on the mountain.

"But we was goin' to town, and by God we was a-goin'. So we went.

"Beyond the crick, farms come out and stopped the desert. From there on I knowed where the wire gates was in the fields. I could tell old man Stefans had put in alfalfa with water from his new well . . . that the widow James was pruning her apricots . . . that such and such a barking dog belonged to Hanky Hanks. Pretty quick I was out onto the Della Road. Town was only half a mile. I could see the sign of the Hearty Laugh Saloon, but old Tony was a-commencin' to loosen behind, the way a pony does when he gives out. For a minute I thought I'd git off and walk him, and then I thought hell, no, if I can't ride into town, I won't go at all . . . and I asked old Tony confidential if he thought he could make it, and he said he reckoned he could if I'd give him time, so we cut down to a walk and it was that way we hit Main Street.

, "Baker's Livery Stable happens to be first on your right. The place was all dark, but I knowed how to git in. I found some axle grease and doctored old Tony and give him a good feed, and then I went on to the saloon. But I took a detour on the way. I wanted to see my girl. It was only eight-fifteen, but maybe I could see her. So at the next street I turned off and went down to the café. I didn't go inside. The place was full, and she was running up and down the tables. I waited there across the street where I could see it all . . . how she'd laugh and smile and make words with her mouth I couldn't hear to these folks she was a-waitin' on . . . and to me they was the luckiest people in the world. Oh, my, she was a sweet-lookin' maiden in them days! . . . pretty face, pretty figure, her foot so light it never touched the ground. But when I seen her serve a plate, I knowed then why it was I'd come . . . I was sick of bein' laid ag'in' the earth at night and bein' rubbed all day by rope and leather . . . I wanted them little hands to touch me. And then I looked at my own hands, covered with axle grease and blood, some Tony's, some of it mine, and I thought . . . 'You dirty hog, you ain't fit to mix with humankind . . . go git yourself respectable.' So I turned 'round and headed for the saloon.

"I can't say just how good that old saloon looked. Them swingin' doors was like the heavenly gates to me, 'cause I come a man a-wearied and blood was on me and my right leg burned like hell's own fire . . . but I had my own idees, and I was on my way, and, when you're thataway, the rest don't matter.

"So I swung inside. There was Jippy at the counter, rolling the boys for a drink . . . there was the green tables and the poker games . . . and I thought . . . 'Well, this is good . . . this is all right.' As I headed up to the bar, I seen an advertisement card saying Jean Harlow was a-gonna play next week in something, and I thought . . . 'By God, I'll do 'er again next Wednesday and take Maxine to see that.' Then I pounds a fist on the bar and calls for Jippy.

" 'Hi, Powder Keg,' he says. 'With you in a minute,' and goes on rolling the bones.

"Well, after five minutes he come, and I was mad.

" 'What the hell, now,' I told him. 'Forgetting old friends?'

" 'Naw,' he says, 'naw. . . .' And then . . . 'Been away?'

"I says . . . 'Gimme a double whiskey.'

"When he come back, I told him to git me a steak, rare, the best in the house. Then I had another whiskey and commenced lookin' for society.

"A bunch of guys was standing there, so I goes over and asks 'em to have a drink with me. Jippy lined 'em up, and we downed 'em, and they kept saying 'OK' and 'Swell,' so I had Jippy line 'em up again.

"Then these guys begun to talk, but not to

me. They was working on a road some place that was cutting the Rocky Mountains in half, and all they could talk about was dough and WPA and CCC and Roosevelt . . . Roosevelt. I didn't want to hear about any of that, so I looked 'round again and seen old Hoopaloo over there at one of the card games.

" 'Come out of that, you old bastard!' I told him, and he come. I set him up a drink and asked him first about Maxine. Yeah, she was fine. Yeah, prettier'n ever. Nope, nobody had beat my time. She'd sure be glad to see me. Been away?

"Well, I said, the hell with you . . . here's my steak, and I'm hungry.

"So I swung 'round and begun to think better of old Jippy just because he'd brought me that steak.

" 'How's Hap?' I asks him.

" 'Dunno,' he says. 'Haven't seen him lately.'

" 'What happened about him and that Seamans girl? I heard her folks was goin' to court over it . . . or that's what a guy told me last week on the mountain.'

" 'Been on the mountain?' he says.

" 'Yeah, I've been on the mountain,' I says.

" 'Well, come to think of it,' he says, 'Hap

did go out of town the other day . . . kind of in a hurry, too.'

" 'Was he ridin' a little cat-hipped sorrel?'

" 'Yeah,' says Jippy, 'believe he was . . . say, wasn't that your horse?'

" 'No,' I says. 'No . . . used to be, but I sold him to Hap.'

"The steak was getting cold right there under my eyes, but I don't know . . . I'd kindy lost my interest. 'Well,' I said, 'this looks like a good steak.' So I cut in, and do you know that steak was just a-turning, just a little bad, like milk, so that you can't decide whether to quit eating or go on. But I stayed with her . . . kindy felt I had to.

"I forgot to tell you . . . all this time somewhere in the back of the room or just outside, I couldn't say right where, they was a noise rising and falling and passing away, like the sound of the wind in them wires. I'd heard it, but I'd been too much on the move to notice, and then it was I made my big mistake . . . workin' on that steak I had a chance to think.

"What the hell was that sound? I stuck my head out the window, but there wasn't no wind. I come back and eat a while. Somebody put a nickel in the phony-graph, and it played a song about 'I Surrender.' Then all of a sudden that wailing sound made itself into words, like the radio does when you tune her in square, and I heard it was a nagging woman. That's all it was . . . just a woman. I eat a while and begun to get indigestion. She was after her old man for something back there behind the wall, poor devil. I feel sorrier for him than any man on earth, and I never even seen him. While listening, I begun to feel the burning of my leg, my face, and a dozen other places I didn't know I had. I wearied fast, but that woman, she never wearied . . . she kept on forever like the wind does in them wires. I couldn't eat no more. Then the phony-graph song about 'I Surrender' . . . it run downhill and quit, and everything in that room flattened out with it. I begun to think about my camp on Aspen Crick . . . just a little thought at first, but she got bigger mighty fast, like a train coming down a track, and then it seemed I wasn't a-getting enough air in that room . . . and how the others laughed and went on playing cards, right in the face of that woman there behind the wall I couldn't see.

"I ordered me another double whiskey, and, when I'd drunk it, I went out of that place.

"I headed back up Main Street. When I come to the street of my girl's café, I kept a-goin', but once I looked. I seen the square of light the big window cut out of the sidewalk, and there come a sound of dishes, suddenlike, when somebody opened a door and went through into the kitchen, and that almost got me 'cause it meant Maxine. But I kept on. I was sour at the roots and couldn't change.

"I went and got Bill Baker out of bed and asked about my little cat-hipped horse, and he said Hap had it over to Joe Petrillo's, so I went and got out Joe, and he told me Jippy was right . . . Hap had rode him out of town, in a hurry. Then I was mad. I went back to the stable and give old Tony another pail of oats and a rub and told him we'd have to travel again . . . and he didn't care much for that, poor devil, 'cause he was a tired horse.

"As we shook out our bridle on the Della Road, day was trying to git over the mountain, but couldn't make it. Old mountain was too much for him, took up all the sky . . . kindy like Jacks in the doorway of the barn, only here I knowed what the mountain had to say 'cause up on Aspen Crick I'd heard him."

Dynamite finished his story. It wasn't like him, but he never asked me if I understood.

As we rode back over the knoll, they switched the lights on in the mill, and I said,

107

pointing: "It's lucky the power line crosses here or you might never have remembered that story."

"Oh, yes, I would," he said. "I can't forget it. I'm married to that girl, Maxine."

# BONAPARTE'S DREAMS

We used to walk away and leave him talking to the empty air, and, when he was alone, he would talk to himself or the cattle and tell them his ideas. We used to talk *about* Bonaparte McPhail. His name was a joke. Sitting in the cookhouse at meals or after supper in the bunkhouse around the potbellied stove, we would carry on, spitting to hear the hot iron sizzle — Derringer who was top hand, Sammy Lee the cat skinner, Jacob, and the rest of us — amusing ourselves with the boners Boney McPhail had pulled.

For instance, one time he was working at a place, and they told him to go out and burn the stubble, so Boney ties some sacks on a wire and the wire behind a wagon, lights those sacks, and just drives around the field. This invention works fine for a while, and Boney is about as proud as Thomas A. Edison until he sees a bunch of heifers in the grain field next door, where they had no business being because that was prize grain and would make thirty sacks to the acre if it made a pound. So what does

Boney do? Why, he gets right over there, wagon and all, and wagon and all he puts those heifers out of that grain — something three men on horseback couldn't do.

Of course, by then he's burnt up eleven thousand dollars' worth of barley, which is why Boney came to California to change his luck and was working on the cattle ranch of Jed Elkins when I knew him, forty-nine years old, drawing a dollar a day and his board, still waiting for his advancement and still thinking too much about Napoléon, Shakespeare, and Thomas A. Edison, who had got him in trouble before. So we carried Boney as a joke and used him to pass the time, until one day . . . and this is what happened.

Jed Elkins's place is up three thousand feet. His valley is a cup inside a rim of mountains that look made of gold. The sun was just coming over those mountains, making them shiny at the edges, when I walked into the blacksmith shop and interrupted Boney who was busy at the anvil.

" 'Morning," he said frostily, glaring through his glasses the way an inventor does who's been interrupted, and kept right on hammering a bar of some kind he had heated in the fire.

Now Boney was not what you'd call beautiful. He looked more than anything like one of those bandy-legged apes that walks like a man: short-legged, long-barreled, rear stuck out, and his blue jeans always were three sizes too long and his dirty gray shirts overlapped them all around by six inches. He sported a felt hat, city-style, that looked as if it had wiped up the floor of some big-city garage, and a cigarette holder, and a brown seep of tobacco juice from the corner of his mouth that was a style all Boney's own.

I said it was time to go feed our cattle. Boney hammered on. He was shaping one of those pinch bars about two feet long made of iron, common to every ranch and carpenter's shop in the country, with a pry on one end and a curved pinch on the other for pulling nails. Boney was building something that looked like a hammer head on the outer curve of this pinch. All of a sudden he stopped, picked up the bar, and went through some wild motions meant to indicate the pulling of a nail with the pinch and the pounding of one in with the hammer.

"Think it'll work?" he asked, handing me his invention.

I made a few passes myself. "Sure it'll work," I told him. "All a fellow needs is an arm and shoulder of iron, and he wouldn't mind using this thing at all."

Boney took back his bar the way a mother takes her baby from a stranger. "Maybe," he said. "We'll see what the board of directors thinks about that . . . yes, sir," he continued, when we had loaded our pickup truck with sacks of rolled barley and cottonseed and were heading up the valley, "yes, sir, I wouldn't be surprised . . . it's been five days now. I wouldn't be surprised to get a letter today from the chairman of the board of directors of the Atlas Steel Company in San Francisco. It's been five days since I wrote and diagrammed him the idea, and, when I'd done that, I went on to explain how there was hundreds of thousands of these pinch bars in daily use throughout the United States, and not a one of 'em but what you had to put it down and pick up a hammer every time you wanted to drive a nail.

"I begged him . . . yes, sir. I begged 'im outright . . . to consider the hours, days, even the years spent and wasted by all the working men multiplied by all the pinch bars, every time that there laying down and picking up occurs. It's a shocker! As I said," concluded Boney, "that was five days ago. 'Course, a board of directors don't meet like you and I. And with ideas like mine there's

112

patents to look up and papers to clear. Oh, it might take a week, maybe longer."

·We drove east toward the mountains. The sun was just rising over the highest peak of all, one somebody of an academic turn had called Olympus, and the name suited because that mountain was a ranch by itself of golden clover and wild oats, marked with lines of green where the sycamore springs ran down and made good growing for the oaks. Jed Elkins turned three hundred head of weaner calves up there each autumn and let them run till they became cattle. They were well on their way, now, and Boney and I had the job of helping them along daily with a little rolled barley and cottonseed and conversation, because, when I wouldn't listen, Boney would talk to them.

"Tell me," he said, and I knew he had got an idea, "you remember bringing them little cattle off Olympus Labor Day for the dehorning? It took four of us all day. Now, if I do the same in an hour, aren't I doing four men's labor?"

"Sounds like you are," I admitted.

"So I do the labor of four men," continued Boney, "aren't I entitled to the wages of them four?"

"Reasonably speaking," I said, "you might be so entitled. Yes."

Boney's cigarette holder worked up until it nearly set the brim of his hat afire, a sure sign his mind had hold of something big. "I'm hittin' Elkins for a raise," he said. "You watch . . . you just watch me now, and I'll show you."

The place we fed the cattle was a hollow in the side of Olympus where a cañon widens and a number of washes come down through the rock. The walls are pitted by the weather into caves where owls live. That hollow itself might be an acre across, and it held, as usual, about a dozen white-faced calves waiting for us.

Boney got excited as soon as he saw them. "H-o-o-o-o, babies!" he cried the familiar greeting. They replied in kind, and he answered them. "Come, babies! How's my babies?" They answered with one voice, crowding all around the pickup: "HUNGRY! HUNGRY!"

This was the conversation Boney carried on with cattle, along with a lot more that only he and the cattle could understand. I would ride through a field, or come over a ridge when he did not know I was around, and would watch and hear him talking to those little cattle, stopping his fence-mending or errand-running, or whatever he happened to be doing at the time, to go and talk with his babies. And they were his babies. Boney had laid his hands on every one of them. He helped them be born. He cut, marked, vaccinated them, and docked their tails. And when the time came for them to leave their mothers and grow up, he would climb the shoulders of Olympus and dig out the springs and fix the leaky troughs with redwood slivers that swell with the water, so that his babies might have something to drink.

Now he got out of the truck to give his general call. He did this like an opera singer, by resting one hand on the fender and swelling up and letting go with a giant's version of what he had been saying: "COME, babies!" And the babies answered and came. From the brakes and gullies, off the slope, up the cañon, from everywhere they came until the sides of Olympus ran red with cattle. This always made Boney shake with excitement. "See, they know me. They know me!" he would exclaim. And yet these were but a small part of the cattle, just the lazier ones who stayed nearby waiting to be fed.

"Now," said Boney, when we had put out our feed into the wooden troughs, "come with me and I'll show you how I can bring in the others! Just imagine you're the boss!"

He led the way up one of those washes that pitch down as steep and bare as the slides in a school yard. We had to lean forward to climb. The rock was of sandstone at first, and then it changed to something harder and darker, and Boney felt his hand along the wall and said with a prospector's smile: "Granite!" We climbed, and again he felt the wall and said approvingly: "Granite. Joshua could have done the job at Jericho alone if he'd had granite like this to help him."

We'd come to a place that was like a chimney leading to the sky and a bright patch of Olympus fringed with trees that you could see away up there in a splash of sunlight. The sight made Boney tell me the story of the two kings and the cloth of gold. These two kings met in a meadow with all their people to declare friendship. They spread a pillow and a gold cloth, standing for Virtue. Then the first king took a glass of wine, standing for the blood of his country, and the second king took another, standing likewise, and they emptied their wine glasses on the cloth of gold till the wine mingled together and ran down. Boney said that was how the sides of Olympus would run with cattle when he shouted.

"I'm a-gonna do it here," he said determinedly, glancing around him like a con-spirator.

"Go ahead," I told him, and he did. He inhaled, he expanded, and then he made the sound, and it was a sound. It flushed the white owls screaming from their caves. It peeled off the face of the stone and sent it crumbling into tiny avalanches. It brought a rock as big as an egg splintering onto the floor of the wash between us, and I shouted — "Boney, that rock might have killed you!" — and he grinned back: "What do you think of my idea now?"

"Fine," I said, still shouting because the echoes kept coming back, "fine . . . you've convinced me!"

He was going to try it again, when I stopped him. There had begun to be a rumble in the wash. The sound was as though a train were coming far away, or per-haps as though water had broken loose somewhere farther up. It grew; it sharp-ened; it became three express trains ready to burst out of a tunnel. I went for one wall and Boney for the other. There was no climbing — a lizard could not have climbed from that wash — so I had to turn and watch the leaders of the cattle come around the bend, pour around that corner in the rock, and begin talking and trying to stop as they saw

Boney, fail to stop, be shoved on down still trying and, in their effort, widening that freshet of cattle till the churning feet were beside my feet, and I could have touched the nearest one. Then they broke on by and were gone in a rumble down the wash. I knew I had started to sweat and that my belly was a pad of dampness.

Then here more came, and more, seeing Boney, trying to stop for him, then breaking and passing on down like so many loads down a coal chute.

At the end there was Boney, grinning and trying to tell me: "You ain't seen nothin'. This here granite's like a pianer scale. You'd oughta see me play her a hundred yards higher!"

"Never mind," I said, "I'll take your word."

We scrambled down to the feed troughs. There was a churning acre of calves, and it took some tall explaining from Boney to tell them why no cottonseed was in those empty troughs. But at last he made himself clear, and we were in the pickup driving home. "You know," he said, "those little cattle are sure fond of me. I wisht I had a couple hundred like 'em to get a start with Verna."

Verna was Boney's widow woman. He met her through the Lonely Hearts Club.

He wrote and asked them for a promising widow of a mind to marry, and they sent him two addresses, one in Santa Ysabel, one in Oakland. He tried the Santa Ysabel one first. The answer came right back. He and the lady quickly discovered an interest in getting married and agreed to meet one Saturday afternoon in the park. At four o'clock Boney was there, in his best new suit and tie. He waited an hour and forty minutes by the goldfish pool, and the only living creature he saw was the large, colored lady on the bench opposite. "She made as if she was gonna approach me, once," he told us afterward, "but it was just scratchin'." But when we kidded him about it, he flared up with genuine regret: "I shoulda spoke to her. She probably was lonesome in her heart just like I was."

When he wrote the second address, Boney asked for a picture, and, when it came, signed "Love, Verna," he showed it around the bunkhouse, and we agreed she must be a widow, all right, because no man could stay married to a face like that and live. Boney thought she was fine. They met downtown in Oakland. She was needing some new stockings at the time, so Boney bought her those. Then it was a new bridge, so Boney arranged that with the dentist.

Finally there were one or two items of insurance to settle, and the wedding day was set for Christmas, which was the day Boney had in mind now, as he told me. "We'll take a herd of heifers, borrow, and calf 'em out to pay the loan. I'll find some city youngster with a rich old man ready to set him up in the cattle business, and he and I'll go partners. Backing's all I need. I got the woman that can put me over . . . really polite, you know, appreciative of them eight-thousand-dollar homes, them beautiful terraces and the rest. Oh, she'll make it easy, as a woman can . . . or she can be ornerier'n buckskin. Cross her once, maybe give her a black eye, and sure as hell she'll go to town shopping the next day, just to get even. But not Verna. . . . Tell me, now, honest," he said, "how much is that steel company gonna give for my pinch bar?"

"Why, I can't guess, Boney," I told him. "I haven't any idea."

"I figure ten thousand," said Boney. "Shucks, what's ten thousand dollars more or less to them big fellers? They don't skimp, that's why they're where they are. And just to show 'em I play the game square, I'll drop the first two thousand right back in their company. And then I'll drop a couple in Standard Oil . . . that's a good company. But the bigger part I'll save . . . I'll start Verna and me with about three hundred little cattle, like them we've left back there."

And so we pulled into the yard just at noon, when Tim, the Chinese cook, was ringing his bell. That dinner bell always made Jingo, the blue Australian shepherd dog, howl miserably, and this gave Boney an idea, so that he broke off what he was saying, thought an instant, and then explained to me. "Know why he howls? Jingo's part Saint Bernard, see? And he thinks it's them monastery bells a-callin' him home."

It had come just before lunch. When Boney arrived, we were all eating, and there it was propped against his coffee mug, the letter. Boney ignored it and sat down.

"See you got mail," said Derringer after a minute. He was top hand. He and Boney never did get along because Boney talked with cattle, and for a bronc' stomper out of Arizona and a master of his art that is like going to church without your pants — it just ain't done.

"Read us your letter, Boney," urged Sammy Lee. "I'll bet Verna has to have a new pair of shoes by Saturday."

"Naw, all of you are wrong," said Jacob,

the irrigator. He kept Jed's alfalfa wet, an old Mormon out of Salt Lake City, and he said: "Naw, sir, it's from the chairman . . . the chairman of the board. And they're all gonna make Boney vice-president, and we'll have to call him 'Mister.' "

So the talk ran, and Boney put his face into his plate and let it go, but he didn't touch the letter. Not until Sammy Lee passed him the coffee. Without thinking, Boney picked up the letter to get at his cup, and, once he had it in his hand, he couldn't set it down.

"Read out," was the word. And Boney did. He read out loud and clear and steady as a judge:

**Dear Mister McPhail:**
**In receiving your last letter, I note the smell of liquor on the flap of the envelope where you licked it. After what happened to my late husband, I told you before I never could marry a man who drinks. Believing you have done this to other women, I am returning your ring by parcel post.**

**Verna H.**

Boney folded up the letter and continued

his meal. There was silence. Then one by one the boys started filing out and finally old Jed, the boss. Old Texas Jed was a kind man. He had the face of a gourd a hundred years old, and he said gently to Boney as he passed: "You fellers burn the upper pasture this afternoon, and clear out them brush piles so we can plow." Then Boney and I were alone, with only Tim out in the kitchen, chippering Chinese to the cats. The clock on the shelf ticked. Boney looked up for the first time, and I thought of faces of animals I had seen go silly and out of shape with pain, as he said, baring his teeth in a silly old grin and shaking a fist at the walls and the world outside: "The combat deepens! On ye brave!" This was not a new saying of Boney's. I'd heard him use it before. It was his version of what Roland had said at the battle of Roncesvalles.

' The field we burned that afternoon was summer-fallow land, running up against Olympus, where some woodchoppers had worked the year before and left their piles of trimmings, dry now and ready for burning before we could plow. Boney and I carried out gunny sacks and old crankcase oil in our pickup, dipped and fired the sacks, and spread them through the piles. Toward mid-afternoon a breeze came up the valley from the ocean and made the fires leap. Soon we were going around in the early winter dusk, and I had not seen Boney for some time, when I met him at a big pyre, leaning on his pitchfork, watching the figures leaping in the flames that live only for a second and are gone. I joined him and looked, too, and finally he said, without turning from the fire: "Michael Archangelo . . . he was a great painter, but he never made statues like those." — meaning the figures in the flame, and then very thoughtfully — "Women has got to be whole hog or none . . . Bob, women has got to be like Caesar's wife . . . out of the question." That was the most Boney ever said to anyone on the matter of the letter.

He and I worked together afterward, while the wind freshened from the sea, turning colder and putting a lid of clouds over the valley. We rounded off and covered the fires against the wind, loaded our tools, and started home with the wind rising beside us through the dark trees in a way that made both wind and trees alive — a kind of edging and building toward something cold and wilder. Then we turned the corner, and I could look back and see the string of red dots shining like rubies in a belt around Olympus. "Our fires, Boney," I said. "The wind brought them alive. We'd better go back."

We stopped the truck.

"Gee, ain't them pretty fires?" said Boney.

"We'd better go back," I told him.

The fires kept winking on and off like fireflies, while we watched, and Boney said that was soldiers passing between us and the fires, although it was only the wind freshening and dying. Finally the lights went out. We waited another ten minutes and drove home.

The last I remember was the sound of Boney, brushing his teeth on the bunkhouse porch where the wash basins are. The next I knew I'd overslept. There was light in the room and sharp voices outside. I got to the window quickly. The light was in the east, just as it should be; but it wasn't daylight, it was fire. The ridge of Mt. Olympus hung up there in the sky like a huge rainbow of flame.

Two minutes later I was meeting Derringer and Jed Elkins by the corner of the barn, and Derringer was saying, as he watched the fingers of that fire take and run: "Not with a horse, you can't," but old Jed was answering him: "We can try, we sure can try to get those little cattle out."

Boney arrived. He was short of breath, missing his hat, and his shirt was not tucked in at all. He took a good look and went off running as though the devil were behind him.

"Where's he going?" Jed demanded.

"Crazy," said Derringer.

"Let's get out the horses," said Jed.

The three of us hit the barn together, and three more came and added to the confusion in the dark, till horses we had known for years were rearing and pulling back and threatening to knock the barn down. There was no rope that would untie, no bridle that fitted, and, if we had forgotten how to swear, we should really have been lost. As it was, we got through.

Somehow we gathered outside, everybody, even Tim in his China-black slippers and beanie hat, saying over and over in a terrible singsong: "Missa Jed, Missa Jed . . . cattle burn all up?" And just as we gathered there at the barn door, a pickup shot by in the darkness, and we had the briefest, wildest glimpse of the face of Boney McPhail, his hair flying, his fist clenched and shaking, and his fighting words: "The combat deepens! On ye brave!" We moved out then.

Boney was far ahead, but we did fairly

well with the help of the wind. It hit us in smearing gusts, and you could feel your clothes flatten to your back and your hat smash down and even the lacing of the horse's tail about your thighs, and then the gust dropped you and did the same to the man ahead. The fire had traced out the main ridge of the mountain. Now a long pincer was nipping out along its base by the farming land, breaking over into one fresh ravine after another where it would take with the draft, like a match set to a jet of gas, and go running clear to the summit. Olympus was being cut into ribbons of flame.

The fire sounded almost alive. You could hear it above the wind, spitting like a big cat on the prowl, mean and ugly and muttering along, until it found a patch of brush it liked and could lick over and relish a minute. It lit everything with a hellish light and roared and muttered and talked among its different parts like a monster, and yet over and above all this you could hear something else, a human voice. It came from the side of Olympus. It might have been old Jove himself up there, calling to hand the thunder and telling the waters to be still. Because you could hear him. You could hear Boney above all the wind and fire, his voice echoing between the summer fallow and the dark sky: "Oooo, babies! COME, babies!"

"By golly," I heard Jed say, "it's Boney!"

I did not try to tell him it was the general call.

Then we rode. The long pincer of that lower flame was pouring over the ridges, hesitating on each crest, gathering like a big snake, and then pouring on over with a lunge and a snapping, backed by the wind. Before we tried to race it, we were beaten. In the cañon where Boney and I had fed the cattle it sent a jet skyward that made Olympus echo and shake, but over it we heard the general call: "COME, my babies! THIS way, babies!"

Then the voice went off short as though a knife had cut.

We stopped riding without knowing why we did. The fire went on across the mountain.

Then we heard a faint sound like the rushing of many wings. Then it was a deep, positive rumble close to the ground as though a dam of water had broken loose. Then here it came in a ragged line breaking through the fire, of shapes of cattle, falling and crying and pressing on, some burning, some already charred, some falling and skidding and showering sparks. They came down, lunging out of that fire like shapes in a dream. They were unbelievable. Their noise was like the cry of terrified children in pain; and they went by and would have run us down if we had not moved, in endless driblets that were agony themselves, dropping off a dead one here and there, smelling acridly of charred flesh and hair like a thousand corrals at branding time; and so on down, a long mass that glowed with its own burning and marked its way.

Far below in the farming ground the herd drew together and circled in a radiant wheel that cried aloud and broke apart gradually to extinguish itself, a section at a time. Derringer blurted out as if he were in pain himself: "Why don't they git apart? Why don't they git apart?" But old Jed answered, as calmly as though he'd seen it every night of his life: "They're rubbin' ag'in' one another. They're rollin' in that plowed land."

At dawn the wind swung into the east and turned the fire back. We watched it die on the ridges and fade away on the slopes where the cattle in October had grazed off all the grass. We heard it whimpering out in the cañons when we set Sammy Lee and Tim rounding up the little cattle that roamed the summer-fallow land still crying, although it was like moaning now — the

129

sound little children make long after what hurt them has gone.

We rode into one cañon with the sun, toward the hollow where Boney and I used to feed cattle. The fire was still burning in the fallen trees, and the walls held and multiplied the heat like metal. We rode over lumps in the trail that had once been cattle. The rising air had killed the owls, too, and they lay dead along the bluffs. A hundred yards up the wash that pitches into the hollow as steep and bare as a slide in the school yard we found what was left of Boney. The fire had not touched him, only the loving feet of his babies. And there he was.

"He'd nearly made it," muttered Derringer. "The poor fool."

"Well, he had an idea," old Jed said thoughtfully.

Jacob added his: "Them city's walls come down, all right, as in the Bible days, but they come down on top o' Boney."

You see, none of them knew you can play a hollow granite wash like you can a piano scale, if you have the knowledge. And they never will believe me when I tell them, although they handle Boney's name differently now. In fact, they have changed the name of Mt. Olympus and called it after him.

# NOBODY DANCED

Jaydee had said he would get Dynamite. This happened Friday afternoon when dust from the big hammer mill settled in his brain and made it ache so badly that he left the feed yard and drove home early to the village where he and Melanie, his young Arkansas woman, had recently set up housekeeping. California hadn't changed Jaydee Jones. He was six solid feet and two inches of Arkansas oak. He was strong — strong as any man in the county his size and weight, but not so strong as the dust hiding in the stems of hay. It made him sick first in his stomach and then in his head, and, as he drove along, he thought how good Melanie would look in the yellow pajamas he had bought for her birthday. He decided to take the next day off, because it was Saturday, and go with Melanie to the motorcycle races in Sacramento.

But when he got home, he couldn't find her. On the table in the front room — the house had two rooms, front and back — was a note somebody had written.

**You're a sweet one, you are. I'll meet**

**ye sometimes else.**

Jaydee's head wasn't any too clear, but he guessed this sentiment wasn't for him, and he recognized Dynamite's handwriting. When Melanie came home, they had hell about it.

Loyetta Mae, wife of Rollo Jane, the Okie, heard them from her trailer house parked in the vacant lot next door. She was getting supper for her husband, who drove a feed truck in the yards. After Rollo and the babies had been fed and put away, she took a basket of laundry — the week's wash of Mrs. Jacks, the foreman's wife, in which were laid first the sheets because they were biggest and then the pillow slips and then the towels and last of all the news she had heard — and drove with it in her 1930 Chevrolet sedan back the two miles to the feed yard.

Mrs. Jacks was a large woman who dressed extensively in beet-colored silk and managed her own affairs. She came onto the back porch herself in answer to Loyetta's knock, being concerned about seven linen doilies that had gone to the wash this week. She had taken in laundry herself at one time and knew how tempting linen doilies can be — even single ones.

132

Next morning Thelma Jenkins, who does the cooking for Mrs. Jacks, went to the cookhouse to borrow an egg from old Mike, ranch cook, and, when we came along at noon to eat our beans, all thirty of us knew Jaydee was going to get Dynamite before we had taken that second mouthful.

By three o'clock, everybody in the yards knew it. At the scale house by the mill, where the boys sit for a smoke on the shady side while their loads are being weighed, Elmer said Jaydee would be with little Dynamite as the hammer mill with a bale of hay: "Grieves me . . . two men fighting over one woman."

Charlie Pell said particularly an Arkansas woman.

Jody said: "Her feet's itched her ever since Jaydee bought her them new shoes."

Cherokee said, if Jaydee'd bought a wedding ring instead of shoes, it would have been a better thing.

So the talk went, and the wind from the sea that blows always in this country carried off the words as it does pollen in the spring and spread them through the river hills, until even the remotest ranchers heard. At quitting time old Boyd Yarrow, who owns a wheat farm in the Happy Valley, stopped me at the barn and said he'd heard Dynamite had killed Jaydee Jones in a gunfight.

"Come to the opera house tonight," I said, "and see for yourself. Sid and Mary Koska are giving the dance."

They don't give operas in Bird Town any more. They've torn down the Palace Hotel and the gingerbread arcades and three of the saloons. But years ago before the railroads came, when the ground was young and an acre put up forty sacks of wheat, Bird Town was a great city. Every autumn grain ships gathered in the river from all the countries of the world and loaded the finest wheat America could give them, and up in Bird Town two miles away the opera girls played every night to a full house.

Now the girls and ships have gone, and the ground has gotten tired, and only Pete who runs the Last Saloon and Abe who runs the grocery can tell you of those busier days. Sid and Mary Koska came from Poland and bought the opera house for three hundred dollars cash and built a partition in the middle so they could live behind it and have their butcher shop in front. And it was here, on this particular Saturday night, that we were going to dance.

In the bunkhouse this made Cherokee get out his best choke-rag, and all through the river hills, in a dozen shanties built of gray-bleached boards, women were putting on those bright polka-dot dresses J.C. Penney sells at $4.98 and bundling up their babies and making sure the kerosene was out and the fire shut up well in the stove.

Bird Town after dark is the best-lighted village in America. It is built at a crossroads where two power lines intersect, and the area of the city as measured by these intersecting lines is exactly seven poles. On each of them an electric bulb is fastened thirty feet from the ground, and these illuminate the seven shanties of the village — and their chicken coops and privies — in a strange way, much as descending flares might light a city ruined in war.

Also there is the Last Saloon, that for these forty years has kept its windows bright, and recently, to stay abreast of the times, Pete has added a new fangle: a red neon letter X which can be seen clear from the fced yard and looks as though the devil himself had marked the place. Actually Pete is no devil. He is a sober man who never drinks himself and listens as patiently to our misfortunes as to the cold marsh wind that for these forty years has talked around the corners of the Last Saloon.

Tonight being Sid and Mary Koska's turn to give a party, their windows cut big yellow blocks from the board porch of the opera house and the dirt and gravel of the country road. Overhead the seven bulbs blazed on their poles, and altogether Bird Town looked as good to us as Broadway, New York City.

First, we heard Jaydee was over at the saloon, had been all day, and that he was beginning to boil. Some of us went over to see. Next, we heard Dynamite inside. It was his music that came out the open door. He played the French harp, the harmonica, and Elmer Lee played the fiddle. They were all the band we needed.

Mary Koska came onto the porch, tapping neatly with her little heels, and called to us: "Come along, boys, and grab yourself a girl." She looked very sweet and trim, standing there against the light with the side of her black head shining and her waist tucked in no bigger than a honeybee's, but the blood in us was cold, and we said we'd be along directly, which meant we had to have a round of Pete's red-eye deluxe.

Ike carried the bottle. We gathered at the end of the porch and watched the people come. Ike said Jaydee's woman wouldn't have the gall to show herself.

"The hell she won't," said Jody. "Keepin' her out o' sight o' mankind is like keepin' bread from butter."

Cherokee said soberly — "Fellers, reckon there'll be a violence done this evening?" — and he sounded like a little boy who's come to a baseball game and just can't wait for it to start.

People arrived, the women carrying the eats: the wrapped-up sandwiches and cookies that would make things easier on Mary Koska. Loyetta Mae led her batch of youngsters past us single file, like a mother duck, and at the tail came Rollo Jane all dressed to pieces and looking very poor. He switched off and came our way and took on a little reinforcement, but Loyetta never looked around. She was a good girl. Ever since '36 when the Oklahoma dust finished her and Rollo, she'd begun to drink a little herself — not much, just a nipper here and there during the day. They said she'd hit it up a little since the baby came. Living in a trailer does get a little slow.

Tex wandered in, long and brown, and Happy Stone and other folk that were Okies the same as Rollo and Loyetta Mae — Laplanders, to be more accurate. That is, they came from where Oklahoma laps over into the United States.

A Cadillac sedan pulled up along the porch, black and shiny as an undertaker's, and that was Jacks and his wife. She drove because it was her car. Jacks used the Company's when he traveled. He got out now, the rough old Arkansawyer, and looked about as comfortable in all that chromium and polish and in his best blue serge as a hickory tree would. Mrs. Jacks wore a hat that wadded up in layers like a honeycomb and carried a cake so big and white it shone clear through its wax paper, and made you swallow hard. Those angel-food cakes of Madam Jacks were heaven cut in ten slices.

At the door Jacks branched our way as Rollo Jane had done. Saturday night he was no boss. He could kick his heels for once in the week and call the square dances and experiment with and explain his favorite subject, which was whiskey.

When the bottle passed him, he opened his mouth wide with a sound like a locomotive letting off steam. "Boys, boys! If I was you, I'd figure they was thousands and thousands of bottles of this here whiskey but I had only one stomach."

"*Arch*-ibald!"

We saw something like a big boulder blocking up the lighted door.

"See you boys d'rectly," said Jacks. "There's my call to sassiety."

We watched him shuffle away, and Cherokee said: "Poor old critter." Then the band hit up "Turkey in the Straw," and we sent the red-eye around again, faster, because our blood was feeling better, and decided it was time to go inside.

When we got there, we saw we'd over-reached ourselves, that liquor'd fooled us like it has so many, because only Sid and Mary Koska were dancing. The rest of the party sat along the wall on benches all on the left-hand side of the room, Mrs. Jacks making a knot in the center with the other foremen's wives and everybody staring straight ahead and saying nothing. Really sociable, it looked. We turned right and lined up along that side of the room, wishing we were back outside. Sid Koska had taken away the meat from his showcase opposite the door and cleaned and swept the space in front of it and the walls, too, but he couldn't very well paint them, and the place looked pretty bare, pretty cold, and all those people never warmed it up a particle. The more they came, the colder it got. Some kids ran around hollering and cutting up, and we watched them just as carefully as if they'd been the most important people in the world and the funniest. Whenever they acted smarty or tripped one another, we'd raise up such a squall as would make your hair stand.

Dynamite did his level best to put some limber in the air. Where the empty show-case met the wall, he flamed in the corner. Right over him was a map of a beef steer showing all the proper cuts. On his left Elmer Lee crooked around a fiddle, causing the catgut to sing in pretty tolerable fashion. But Dynamite, he was made of music. He had a harmonica fastened to a barbed-wire holder, chuck-wagon style, that kept it close against his mouth and left two hands free for the guitar. His dark red hair boiled up in curls; he wore a shirt the color of wine, and his white hands flashed across it as they played the strings. He swayed and stamped and chewed that little harp as though it were an ear of corn, and music grew right out of him and filled the room.

But nobody danced — that was Dyna-mite's trouble.

When Jacks finally noticed us standing in some misery along the wall, he sang out: "Everybody dance!" That meant a Paul Jones and a chance to mix it up a little and warm the spirit. We spread around in a circle, and, when the band led away with "Red River Valley," we followed, weaving in the ladies' chain from hand to hand. Slip and slide, it went, and slip and slide. If your feet are working, your face doesn't feel so bad. When the little ladies took our hand and smiled, we were ready.

"Dance with the gal *be*-fore you!" was the call. It paired me off against Maxine, Dynamite's wife. She gave me a dutiful smile, because we were friends, and went on chewing gum. She looked like a fierce doll. For over a year now, ever since the baby came, she hadn't had the money for a permanent, and her black hair was running more to strings than braid. She'd made the brown dress she wore, and she was fiddling around behind it now with one hand at a green sash that had come undone. She had on brand-new slippers of the purple shade you see on certain kinds of lamps. They cost her $3.49 out of Monkey Ward's in Oakland. Or $2.49 — she told me, but I forget. I tried to make her talk, but her eyes went away over my shoulder and found Dynamite, not proudly or very cheerfully — just because they had to.

Dynamite got the ladies' eyes, but, when he got the rest of them, they worked. The hand I held in mine was hard as the sole of a shoe.

Maxine asked to be let go. Through all that racket she heard something I never did and hurried, wobbly on her high heels, to what used to be a coatroom of the opera house. In the old days, if you wanted to be swell, you could check your hat here as you came in. Tonight it was a nursery — no light, no furniture. Laid along the floor were bundles of that precious white and pink that couldn't be left at home, and I saw Maxine pick up one of them and hold it tight against her narrow chest as a child might cuddle a doll.

Melanie Jones came into the room just then. Without looking, we all knew this. She wore a black dress that fitted to her small round body in a way that made your eye come back. Her breathing was deep and slow, as though maybe she had run a bit, and this flushed her oval face and barely parted her lips and made her pale eyes dance and sing — the whole picture was framed with little golden hair.

Mary Koska led her to a sink in the corner, behind the heavy wooden table where Sid does his butchering, and offered her a glass of beer, but Melanie didn't want beer.

"A whiskey?" said Mary sweetly, laying her hand on the girl's shoulder. "A little gin, dear?"

Melanie took a quick glass of gin and washed it down with water from the tap. Then Mary cracked open the door into the back of the house, and the two of them leaned through and drew faint cheers from the poker game. Ike and Jody, feeling their oats, waltzed up behind, pretending to be very smart, and caught each girl around the waist and swung her away, laughing.

Over on the bench Mrs. Jacks and the foremen's wives tied their heads together.

Jacks took his coat off, stopped the music, and announced the time had come to square dance.

"Mother," he said to Mrs. Jacks, who still wore her hat, "take off that beehive and dance with your old man."

Mrs. Jacks wanted to look lady-like and severe, but couldn't manage it and blushed, exactly the way she used to in the sixth grace of the Hickory Bend Grammar School when Jacks carved her initials on his desk. But she would not dance, and she looked dark, indeed, when Jacks led Melanie Jones onto the floor.

Three couples joined him — Jody and Mary, and the Happy Stones, and Cherokee with Maxine.

"Oh, hold 'er tight," Jacks squealed. "Oh, hold 'er right. Oh, *hold* 'er tight!"

The music broke full speed into — "She'll be comin' round the mountain when she comes, when she comes. She'll be drivin' six white horses when she comes." — as though the band had suddenly boarded a train.

Feet began to polish the floor. Jacks squealed the way to go.

**Left foot up**
**And right foot down**
**And meet yore honey**
**Go 'round and 'round . . .**

Back and forth that shuffling circle wove, broke, and built itself again.

**Inside out**
**And outside in**
**And eight hands up**
**And a-goin' ag'in.**

The music poured along monotonous as running water and just as strong. It got inside those shuffling feet and told them where to go — Jacks could have saved his breath. It got inside all the dancers and led them as a stream does straws, slowly, quickly, gone suddenly from here to there. In the center of the room they made a weaving eddy. Maxine began to laugh. Her green sash came untied behind, but she didn't notice. When she finished "Chicken in the Bread Pan," Cherokee caught her by both hands and swung her off around the room, and she flew in a brown whirl, laughing like a child pushed high on a swing.

Melanie floated on the face of the music. She fed herself upon it secretly, as a soft cloud builds in the sky. She didn't see her partner, Jody, or any of the people in that room, but only something far away that kept her lips parted just a little and brought a smile around the edges of her face — a funny kind of smile that wasn't there when you looked right at it.

I saw Dynamite watch her as he would a filly that he meant to break. We around the wall began to stamp and squeal. The poker game broke up behind the partition and gathered in the door, and most of their eyes were for Melanie. Youngsters who had been asleep woke up and cried, but nobody heard them. A very strange thing happened. That room itself began to change. Boards, windows, faces, silver hooks for meat behind the counter ran together in the music and seemed made of yellow light, and all of them went around and around with a stamp and a squeal and a stamp and a squeal. Only Melanie's pale eyes kept separate and looked far away.

When Jaydee came into the room, she simply closed them and went on dancing.

We hushed our noise suddenly, but the music and the shuffle of the dance went on, and the room sounded like a train does when it enters a tunnel. Jaydee stopped inside the door and balanced back and forth, and you could hear him breathe. He was all flushed and spotted, and he looked mean — mean as a big dark tree that's going to fall on somebody. He stared and stared at Melanie as though he'd never seen her in his life before, and soon the music had him swaying in the proper time, but shakily, because he was drunk.

Jacks's face shriveled like a piece of ground in winter. Even the air was cold in that room, but he pretended not to notice and went on calling and calling until he sounded far away, like a man shouting in a valley. Melanie kept her eyes tightly shut, and Jaydee stared as if he'd make her open them.

Then a string of Dynamite's guitar broke with a *ping*.

The party was over.

In one lurch Jaydee had crossed that floor. He kicked twice at the toe of Dynamite's boot.

"Are ye man enough?" he said.

Dynamite smiled. He didn't come to Jaydee's shoulder, but he laid down the guitar, and it made the faintest musical echo.

Jacks said: "Boys, we're guests in this house."

Jaydee headed for the door, with Dynamite behind him, and I thought, if he was Arkansas oak, then Dynamite was one of those cats that can live in a tree. He wouldn't fight only to hit, but with tooth and claw and anything that came in handy. He wore new spurs, I saw, that lifted brightly as he walked along.

They got to the open door, and there a scream met them that was cold as murder.

"Bitch    dirty bitch!"

Outside in the ring of light beyond the porch Melanie was flat on the edge of the road. Maxine stood over her holding a slipper — a purple slipper. She let Melanie get up on hands and knees and then knocked her down.

"Jesus Christ!" said Jaydee.

A spot was blossoming on Melanie's neck red as a bullet hole. She gathered suddenly and tried to tackle Maxine.

This time the slipper aimed for the tender piece of neck behind the head, the place a child can kill a steer, but Melanie came too fast, and the sharp heel bit between her shoulder blades where the dress parted to show her soft back. She went skidding in the dust, both hands reaching for Maxine. They barely caught the hem of the brown dress and clung there for a long second that made your sweat come cold to see it, while the slipper rose and fell. She put her face up once, and the slipper put it down. Then with a quick jerk Maxine toppled.

The two of them rolled there in the dust like a couple of dogs.

Dynamite squeezed past Jaydee and jumped the steps; Jaydee followed but tripped over the rolling bodies and fell like one of those giants in a story book. Dynamite got Maxine by the arm. She bit the back of his hand, and he let go and called her a bitch, holding his right hand with his left. Jaydee got a hammer-lock on Maxine from behind and tore her loose from Melanie and carried her off, screaming, beyond the rim of light. Melanie stayed down in the dirt, crying into it. Dynamite knelt over her, very white.

"Honey," he said, "don't cry."

She raised her face, stringy with hair, gashed all red by the slipper, and put it up against the cowboy's knee and cried and cried. He pulled a blue silk handkerchief from his hip pocket and tried to wipe away the blood, but it mixed with the tears and dust and made a dirty stain on the girl's face.

"Now you've got to get up," he said. "Come on . . . that's right."

He helped Melanie to stand and brushed off some of the dust. He wiped her face again, and this time got it clean, although the blood came welling out again. He called to Mary Koska: "Mary, will you take her home?"

Off in the dark we could hear Maxine screaming, telling Jaydee about himself.

Mary came down the steps, and she took and comforted Melanie as if this was her own child, and Melanie, still crying, bent half over, put her head deep in Mary's side, and cried and cried as she was led away.

Maxine never had stopped screaming, but she sounded muffled now, like a bad girl shut in a closet, and we knew Jaydee had locked her in a car somewhere.

When he came back inside the light, he was rubbing his face with both hands, as though maybe he would like to wash it, and then he saw Dynamite and snapped up straight. There he stood, and there stood Dynamite with the yellow circle in between where the ripped-up ground was and a piece of Melanie's black dress. Their eyes met for a second. Cherokee on the porch coughed, and it sounded like a gun going off, and then Dynamite started across the circle, and

149

Jaydee put his feet apart and watched him come.

Dynamite walked quickly, right up to Jaydee, and took him by the arm.

"How's your woman?" he said.

"Why . . . she's OK," Jaydee said. "She's . . . OK. How's your'n?"

"Same," said Dynamite. "What say we go over to Pete's and wash it down?"

"Sure," said Jaydee. "Yeah, that's a good idea."

They turned together, those two husbands, and started off across the road, and the seven lofty streetlights pinched their shadows down no bigger than two boys. Bird Town became silent all at once. Maxine had stopped her screaming. From behind us Jacks called out: "Everybody join hands. We got a dance here, don't forgit."

So we all went back inside, and after a very little while, with only Elmer's fiddle, we made that old opera house shake and sing as it hadn't done since the grain ships lay in the river and the girls rolled long black stockings in what is now Mary Koska's pantry. Even Mrs. Jacks danced, with Jacks, which was the second most important thing to happen that evening.

# JIM MAGEE'S SAND

The year Atlas Steel hit 110 and Masterson Securities refinanced and came out with some gilt edge debentures at 6.5, the year the wind of Pelican Island blew his cattle into the sea and Melanie Jones danced in a meat market and Uncle Arky Billy fought the Duke, T. S. Ordway attended one meeting too many. It didn't happen all at once; it was gradual business, building up and building up until all of a sudden he was absent, and we didn't see him any more around El Dorado Investment Company.

All we got was word of him — by phone, by wire — although sometimes on the summer evenings, if you walked alone from the bunkhouse among the pens of cattle when the light blew in low from the bay over ripe grain, you would hear the soft crunch and mutter of a heavy car, and a big Lincoln would slide past and give you just a whiff of good cigars and the glimpse and echo of big things in the making — those little words that break the ground before ever the boys in the bunkhouse take their picks and go to work.

However, word or man, the cattle in the pens continued to grow fat, and the grain prospered, and, if you had flown the plane that comes over every afternoon at four, nine minutes out of San Francisco for New York, you would have seen the feed yard down below like a dark red stain on the earth. You would have seen the arm of the slough reaching among the cattle, and the ribbon of the river end and frazzle out among the delta islands to make a bay.

We had a lot of rain that year. It began early in December, raining four or five days a week, and by Christmas we were watching the river and the levees. The yards turned to gray paste that oozed away in layers down the alleys. The cattle stopped eating and stood all day huddled against the fences where the rain drifted them. Men and dogs got up early and stayed wet, and three times every week T. S. Ordway telephoned from El Paso where he'd traveled on a deal to get some Mexican cattle shipped across the border, and to buy and sell a couple of banks in his spare time.

So it was the morning before New Year's when Barb, my chunky sorrel, and I turned down Mill Alley square into a southeast gale that humped our backs worse than it did the cattle's, and blew a thin rain up the slough.

Outside the bay was choppy.

We stopped on the knoll above the beet-pulp pit, which looks like a stadium filled with stale, shredded coconut, warm and steaming, and watched a dragline crane bucketing the pulp from a barge that was tied in the slough against the pit. Down there in the alley stood a black pickup truck, which meant only one thing: trouble *and* Jim Magee. Those two went together. Whenever anything got wrong, you sent for the scavenger bunch, and first Jim would come in his black pickup, an omen of disaster, and then his crew of roustabouts and handy-men — all ages, shapes, and sizes — perched like a flock of vultures around the edge of a flat-bed truck. There wasn't anything they couldn't do, with Jim to lead. He was Ordway's construction foreman, black Irish, six feet long and two feet wide — a carpenter, blacksmith, mechanic, plumber, even a shipwright, for he had worked in the Navy Yard and knew all about boats and how to caulk and repair barges. And so he had charge of the giant crane and the four Company barges that hauled beet pulp night and day. All the water pipes on the ranch were laid by Jim and dug up by him when they leaked, and only he knew where the mains ran under the ground and which valve to turn when you wanted the water shut off in Mill Alley.

Barb and I went down Mill Alley, cutting the wind, and got about even with the truck when up came Jim himself through one of the holes in the side of the pit where men go down to the drains at the bottom. He lay flat again and began lifting on something just out of sight that was a little too much for him. I got off and lent a hand, and we lifted out one of those Jaeger pumps that push the rain and beet juice out of the pit.

"What's the trouble?" I said.

"Carburetor cracked," said Jim, pointing — that hand was knotty-red and the arm brown and hard as the bole of a tree. Jim wore what he did every day: shirtsleeves, brown canvas breeches tucked in knee boots, and a rain hat that was extra. Also he had something he never went without: a ball-peen hammer slung through a loop on his trouser leg. I wondered how he had got the pump up thirty feet from the bottom of the pit, because it was a fair weight for two men.

"Feeling kind of waspy today?" I asked.

"Yeah," said Jim, looking right at me with those bare blue eyes so that I never could tell whether he wanted to laugh or fight. "Yeah," he said, "these days, whenever it rains, I eat an extra plate of beans," and he gave a wave behind him toward the river. I knew he meant the levees. T.S. hadn't doctored them this autumn as he should. He had meant to. Jim had been after him about it, and T.S. had hell here once before, years ago — 1918, I think it was — when the sky broke open for a whole month and the river ran and his was the only levee to hold. He did it then himself — skinned a six-mule team — with baled hay rustled from the warehouse. But that was years ago when T.S. didn't have so many meetings.

"When is it due?" I asked Jim. I meant the tide. Along near Christmas, when the days are shortest and the moon a certain way, something happens to the tides and, if they back up in the bay against a southeast wind and the river is coming down, then watch out.

" 'Bout five," said Jim. "Four fifty-five, I think. Let's have a look now and see how she stands."

We took off around the end of the pit and came along the dock where the dragline engine roared and the wind howled through the planking and nearly blew us off into the slough. We hung over the side and saw a big white ruler fastened to one of the piles, where the water stood above the number 7.

"She's ebbing now!" screamed Jim.

She would be in at five — nine-feet-six, the highest of the year.

We looked down past the mill where the angle of the levee fringed with tules held six thousand head of cattle between the slough and the river.

"I don't like it," said Jim, and then: "Ever buckaroo on water?"

"What do you mean?" I said.

"Swim?" said Jim.

"Come on," I said, "*come* on . . . !"

"You god-damned cowboys got a barge of cattle coming this afternoon, feeder steers from Mandeville."

"Well?" I said.

"Well, hell," said Jim. "I canceled my pulp barges today. You let yours get away early, and we can't catch her now."

I looked at the slough. "You mean a barge won't fit in here this afternoon?"

"I mean that," said Jim. "And if a barge does, chances are the river will, too. But," he said, "they're your cattle, not mine. I'm not cattle boss, am I?"

"You son-of-a-gun," I said, "you're vice president around here, and you know it."

Jim gave me a shrug and a gesture of the hands that passed all title to the howling wind and the water rising in the slough.

"We don't need a vice president," he said. "We need a levee."

And then he struck off along the dock to see what Big Bill Williams was doing with the dragline.

At noon we heard the river was three feet above flood at Pride's Landing. At one o'clock she hit Brownsville and ran over, and they opened the Battle Island by-pass to save the levees lower down.

Midway on our afternoon round, with the wind sharpening all the time and the rain beginning to feel like pellets of lead, Barb and I met Jacks in Office Alley. He told me to get wire cutters from Tony at the shop and to go to the river and stand by in case we had to take the cattle out in a hurry.

When I crossed the knoll above the mill, I could barely see the river through the rain — an ugly, swollen thing like a big, brown arm that's got infected. The open two or three miles to the Appleton shore was lathered into whitecaps all the way, looking more like blood than water. Six thousand cattle were a reddish smear and Jim Magee's men black dots, scrambling around in the mud.

A truck passed, loaded with sand, then two more full of light gravel.

I turned into Long Alley, which runs between pens for a mile and a half to the river. Over on the levee men were keeping out the slough with shovels. You could hear them shouting faintly as though they were a mile away instead of a hundred yards.

Away down at the elbow of the levee, where the slough opens off the river, a bull-dozer tractor was stuck; and, when I got closer, I saw Jim Magee was there and Jacks and Dynamite, my pard. Waves smashed over them high as a house, but nobody minded the river. A muddy line of men was passing bags of sand for fifty yards along the slough, like an old-fashioned bucket brigade, to a low place where already a lake of water had seeped through into the pens. Others filled the bags as fast as trucks could bring the sand. Every able-bodied man was on that levee.

The cattle stood around and watched, in water over their knees and very serious and quiet, like a lot of sober old veterans.

The waves were sending spray in jets and gobs and forked tongues like white fire; it mixed with the rain and wind and hit those little men around the bulldozer so hard they seemed to be sewed up in a white border of some kind. Jim had another tractor, a big R D-7, on the end of the bulldozer and a couple of trucks rigged in tandem by their chains; and, when he gave the signal, all that line of metal went to pulling like a big freight does on a hill, and out came the bulldozer like a rabbit from a hollow log and ran on backwards fifteen yards before Jim could get her stopped.

Just then I bumped into Dynamite in a Company raincoat about thirteen sizes too large, that dragged the ground as he walked.

"Hey!" he shouted, his face very red from the rain. "She's a rip-snorter and a vinegar roan! Why didn'tcha bring a boat?"

A wave came over, blotting him out, making the ground shudder and go down and up, like a man hit hard on the jaw.

"We're hopin' the jelly will hold!" sang Dynamite. "It was only T.S. put her here. Looks like God Almighty'll take her away!"

Then out of all the time in the world, one of those things happened that sometimes does: the grandfather of every wave that ever rose hit that river levee, and, I'm telling you, it rocked the cattle on their feet. I started to run. I thought I saw the ocean coming. Dynamite started, too, but, when he saw me, he stopped and began laughing, and then the wave came down out of the sky with a slap and knocked him flat and sent him skidding up the alley like a log on a beach.

It left him and went back, and with it a big chunk of the levee.

Jim Magee was just unhitching his bulldozer over on the slough. He never made a sign, just got aboard and came our way, dodging around his own black pickup and peeling off the levee with him and leaving it in the hole — just a morsel for the next big wave to tear away. But he came again, and with him boards and barrels and the trash of twenty years collected on that levee — some old gray bales of hay that looked as if they'd been there since T. S. Ordway stopped the river back in '18.

He took time to stop the sand trucks coming down Long Alley and made them dump their loads and sent them back for heavy gravel. Then he really went to skinning that cat. He slung mud from those flying tracks farther than the river spray and faster, till he was beating those big rollers to every punch, and the cut in the levee began to heal.

Half an hour and he had her done, spun the big cat on a dime, flirting its tail at the river, and rattled over to the slough. He'd never bothered his men at all; they'd wasted time just watching.

It was getting dark. Dynamite and I hurried to the levee to see Jacks, while the wind smacked our clothes against our skin and took our breath away and kept shoving in those ugly brown rollers as though it wanted to finish us off before dark.

Jacks said wait a while about the cattle, the old man was coming. I never blamed him. Six thousand head of cattle are not easily moved in the first place, get clear off feed when they are, and lose pounds and time and money — all that in addition to the mix-up. So we waited.

Four-twenty, it was, when Dynamite nudged my arm, and I saw a long, black limousine slide down the alley — a Lincoln, which meant only one thing: T. S. Ordway himself. The chauffeur didn't know us, but we got a wave from old T.S. He always had a word for the boys; he was good at words, that old operator.

Jim Magee was busy, but Jacks gathered around, and even old Reuben Child, the lame cowboy who never missed a doings that had cattle in it, came hobbling on his cane out of the dusk.

T.S. didn't leave the car. It wasn't like him. Years ago he would have been out there, lending a hand on the levee, skinning a pair of mules himself, putting muscle as well as words into it, but the years had gone and left him at his desk with a paunch, a little sag around the corners of his face, gray hair, glasses, plenty of good clothes.

He held a meeting at the window of the car, and its matter was simply this: cattle in or out. Old Rube began to wave his cane after a spell, and you could tell where he stood, but the others knew better; they outvoted him, and the cattle stayed.

Fifteen minutes and the tide would start downhill. Maybe on paper it looked all right, but outdoors it's different. You can't tell all the things a southeast wind can do in fifteen minutes when there's a river and a tide to help.

I'm here to say the wrath of God came down to earth that quarter hour in December, 1940. First, lightning broke the sky and came into our valley, and even the rain stood still. For a second you could see a hundred miles, and everything was stuck, jaundiced, the hills shrunk. You didn't want to look, but you had to. Night fell on one gust of wind. Then everything got bigger. Those little, three-inch waves lapping in the slough, where all the storm couldn't reach, were big enough to sink a house. They were the tide. Like death, you couldn't see it. There was only one wind on earth and one river and one human being which was you — nobody else mattered.

I had tied my pony. Barb reared now and broke away and ran off up the alley. It was time to run.

You just could see the line of men along the slough, with weather passing in between so fast that that muddy line seemed hardly to move. It looked slow, a thousand miles away, but it moved, it had life, and all the wind in the sky and all the rivers of earth couldn't stop those Okies, Arkies, Dutchmen, and Swedes. . . . They stayed with her, although, if you'd asked them why, they couldn't have said. It wasn't for T. S. Ordway, not altogether for Jim Magee — just to win. And they fought and scrambled and slung those bags until lights moved upstream on the water.

"She's here!" somebody screamed.

I looked and looked till the wind stung shut my eyes. When I opened them, there was the shadow of the cattle barge, like a dark building two stories high, and ahead of it one hawser-length the tiny shadow of the tug. Red and green lights were on its deck house. Now and then a wave building up in shore would put them out completely.

T.S. and Jacks broke out of the Lincoln at a run.

We followed.

Jim Magee, coming from the left, met us

at the elbow of the levee where the slough takes off the river.

"Jim!" said old T.S., "we can't have that barge in here. She'll flood the yards. I telephoned from Stockton for a motor barge to stop her. Jim, I want you to send a boat out and tell the captain he can't come in here!"

I looked at the river and felt a little sick at my stomach.

Jim didn't have an answer.

We stood there in the rain, leaning forward as if we could see better that way and think better, and you could feel the seconds going by, the motion of that storm and water and the barge coming down so fast.

One of Jim's boys splashed up out of the dark, said something, and Jim repeated at a yell: "Mister Ordway, did you hear that? She's over now . . . the slough is over now in a place sixty feet wide!"

This time T.S. didn't have an answer.

From faraway there came the snort of cattle, sharp, anxious — the one they make, not when they're playing or hungry, but only when they've nosed into something strange they don't like. I could see the dark water creeping out around their feet as clearly as if I'd been right there. T.S. started — "Jim. . . ." — but Jim had spun away into the night.

We tried to see where he went and ended up looking in each other's faces.

The tug was edging for the slough, quartering the gale, and T.S. sounded like a man about to die when he said, too quietly: "Funny he doesn't use his searchlight."

' Was she coming or was she not? In the pale, shimmery light that darkness brings over water you could see the barge clearly for a second, stuck in such cross-currents of wind and tide, crested with so much white foam, that she seemed to move hardly at all. Then she blotted out. It became plain she wasn't coming for the slough. She had passed the turning and was headed on straight down.

Old Rube said: "Bless me, gracious!"

T.S. kept his opinion.

We couldn't figure where the barge would land. As we wondered, she started swinging off shore, square into the wind, straight across the flood and incoming tide, and, when the wind took her, she stopped still, and that tug on the end of its chain leaped and staggered like a dog chained to a wall. Then slowly, little by little, it crept ahead.

The last we saw, the barge lay off into the southeast like a sunken reef, with the spray arching clear over her and the Appleton shore three miles away.

"Well," said T.S., and swallowed his

upper lip, "there goes three hundred head of yearling steers somewhere. They're not ours till they're on the dock . . . that's the agreement." He and Jacks discussed the barge company, the amount of insurance it usually carried, and suddenly they remembered the break in the slough levee and called for Jim Magee, but there was no Jim. They discussed, waited, finally started out.

Far up the river, lights came back. In a minute she was plainly seen — tug and barge riding the wind, heading for the slough's mouth as fast as the gusts of rain.

"It's the barge," said T.S.

"By God it is," said Jacks.

"It's the barge all right," said old Rube.

"No searchlight," said T.S. "I don't understand . . . ," but he never finished that one. I didn't let him. The sneaking hunch had taken me that no captain of any cattle barge on earth could snake his load in blind out of that kind of river that time of night. If he had a light, where was it? I looked behind, and then I hollered: "The pickup! Watch the pickup!" Jim was signaling; his lights blinked on and off.

T.S. started for him at a run.

The barge was at the mouth of the slough.

"Jim!" The wind brought it back to us diluted *"Jim . . . !"*

The barge was in.

Jim moved the pickup to keep his lights in view, and T.S., who was beating on the glass, slipped and went flat in the mud.

Jacks ran to pick him up, and Dynamite and I took off along the levee.

Once the barge hit the far side and stuck a minute. We gained and got ahead.

She wasn't fifty feet away.

We heard the water gurgling at the break as Jim overtook us.

His men were there, still trying, wading in the dark apron of water that slid over into the pens, plopping down, one at a time, sacks that made splashes like pebbles thrown into the sea.

"We're gonna moor the barge across the gap," sang Jim. "Grab the forward line and tie to as many fence posts as you can."

Even in the dark you could hear the mutter of dissent: "What the hell now? Magee's gone nuts!"

"Watch out!" yelled Jim. "Watch out for the big wave."

The barge loomed over us in the night, big as a battleship, and a wave we never saw knocked us to our knees. Then she hit with a thud and stuck. Dynamite had a line and was looping it on one fence post, then a second, then a third, before she loosened in the mud and slid ahead, and the first post came up stickily like a tooth being pulled. But the tug was churning on the offside, and we had her fast against the bank.

This was good, but not enough. Thirty feet of water slid past the stem and over into the pens, faster and faster in the narrow space, and the sand was far away.

Jim began wading out. He tripped once, and I thought he had washed away into the pens, or had sunk down into the mud — that levee's full of holes — but he made a quick stagger and got through.

Then he was gone, and we had the water.

Sammy King came up, Jim's straw boss, and half a dozen men with bags of sand. The water on that thirty feet was knee-deep, but it might have been a hundred. We threw in bags and boards and mud, handfuls of tules, but it all went away with the dark water, and you could hear the bags go splash and tumble down beyond, into the pens, and the sloshing of the cattle moving with them. We went in shoulder to shoulder, hand to hand, making the water break around us, slapping at that dark apron with our boards and shovels. I saw the water find a hole and rim it out and suck into it with a sound like a man strangling to death, until that little hole became a pit and then a gash and then a ragged wound in the side of the levee.

Sammy King and another guy and I joined hands and went down in up to our knees, then our thighs, but the ground slid away under us, and they hauled us out, spitting sand and water, damning.

We saw two figures coming — Jacks and old T.S.

"Stay with her, boys," the old man said. "Stay with her now, you've got her!"

We cussed him under our breath.

Something moved and slipped in the darkness overhead, along the deck of the barge, and came on over into the water with a sucking splash. I thought it was a bag of sand. When the ripples quieted, I saw it was a yearling steer.

The tug had got its searchlight going. The big beam came to us in blinding yellow stripes and flashes, across the rain, through the railings of the barge as the tug rocked on the water. You could see the beeves stowed in like sacks, gray and muddy, and the deckhand crouching by the capstan pulling something, all come and gone in a flash; and then there was another figure, a great big shadow of a guy standing among the cattle with a hammer, a heavy ball-peen hammer, smacking out their brains as though they were so many ten-penny nails.

"Why, he's killing the cattle!" said T.S. and just stood there.

Then we got busy.

, We caught those yearling steers and laid them in the gap; we poured and filled them in like mortar between the barge and the levee. We were masons that night — stonemasons who worked in flesh — and we built a wall such as no men ever built before. It was like the Bible's description of the last great battle of the world, when the living shall walk upon the dead, because many of those steers Jim hadn't killed, and they died slowly till we found them.

, We used our bars and shovels. You'd go along and feel the ground move under you and that would be a muscle dying, a hind leg usually. Once I put my foot into a hole and went down deep in something warm, and, as I rose, part of the ground came with me like a shadow. There was a shape there worse than death — horns and eyes and blood and mud. It moved. I had a shovel with me; I smashed it down and got it under water, but it came again, and I had to smash and trample till the apron of the break ran smooth.

Like bricks we added them and stuck our bars and shovels in behind for piling, and our knees, till the pressure of the flood grew weaker, and the wall could stand alone.

Things moved fast. We got to talking short and silly as men do sometimes when they've got a lot to win. "Pass the sirloin, Johnny!" was the word for more beef on the line, and "Jim Magee's sand" was another — "Magee's sand, worth fifty bucks a bag!" And so it came to be known through all the West wherever men knew a horse from a cow, and that's a lot of country.

After I don't know how long, Sammy King called to Jim to hold it.

Far to the north thunder was growling as though it still wanted to come back and get us. We could hear the cattle in the pens still going with the water. But no more water would come; we'd rolled up that apron.

We stood around, tamping down a little and filling in, knowing we had done something big and getting ready to tell each other about it, but still relishing the story in our minds. Before we'd decided on just the right words, Jim Magee came along the levee, dark in his rainclothes, narrow at the top and wide at the bottom like the shape of a tree. He came on one side, Ordway and Jacks stood on the other, and of us all that had been thinking of good words only T.S. found any to say. "Jim!" he pealed out, "Jim boy, that was a fine piece of work, a great piece of work. Here, let's have a drink on it!"

He brought out a silver pocket flask, undid the cork, and passed it across to Jim.

Magee looked like a kid at Christmas time who's been handed a great big expensive toy he doesn't want. He knocked his hat back with one hand, raised the flask with the other, then brought the first hand down and wiped off the nozzle, then he pulled. The flask went around the circle and back to old T.S., but by that time it was empty.

Nobody had thought of just the right word, although it was quiet now, the wind and rain having gone away with the thunder. A flash came all of a sudden from the tug's searchlight, and T.S. was cut out of the darkness and given to us to remember, standing there alone, all sopped and muddy, with an empty flask. He was on one side; we and Jim were on the other.

"Well," said Argo, the radical Slav, the one we called "Communeeste," "well, by God, I guess that's her!" and reached into his shirt pocket for a cigarette.

# THE LEGEND OF SHORM

One evening after supper Shorm, with sudden change of mood, said to the old *ranchero:* "Look here, Porfirio, I didn't come to California from Texas to die of the drought in a back cañon. I came here to capture that wild bull, and, if I can't catch him, why, I'm not going to stay around and shrivel away by inches just to suit you!"

It was their first controversy in months of being together. During those months Shorm had tried his best to rope the black outlaw bull and failed; he had seen his best catch dog stamped like a rag into the hillside. Porfirio had patiently looked on, knowing the outlaw was uncatchable. Then the drought came. It burned the Santa Rita hills to cinders. The gentle cattle were taken out of the country. Most of the Anglo stockmen went with them. Now Shorm and Porfirio were alone like two relics in Porfirio's tumble-down *hacienda* in the cañon. The creek had turned into sand, the once grassy hills to dirt. Nights like tonight the ranges piled one on top of the other like heaps of ashes under the moon. Porfirio stood at the window, watching the moonlit yard. Shorm had raised himself on one elbow on his rawhide bunk. Much younger, he had always deferred to Porfirio, but he did not feel like doing so tonight.

"You are free to go," Porfirio replied. "There is the coast." He swept his arm toward the west.

"You know I won't go and leave you here. Let me put a bullet through that bull and our troubles will be over. I know you're staying just for him. You're sentimental, Porfirio. He's the last black Spanish bull. You're the last Spanish *ranchero*. Excuse me for speaking so frankly, but at times like these a fellow's got to. You can't stay on here longer. There's not enough water in the cistern now to keep a frog alive. And the feed in the barn's 'most gone . . . that old pile of moss you call feed. Those horses won't have strength to carry us a week from now. Let's take 'em and go, while the going's good. Or else let me put a bullet through him. Then I think the rains *will* come!"

"Would it be fair?" Porfirio turned around and repeated in his musical Castilian voice, soft with the aristocratic lisp he had inherited from his forebears and which generations of New World living had not eradicated. "Would it?"

"By golly, anything's fair in times like these!"

"Listen. . . ."

"I know! He'll be in the room with us next!"

It was the footsteps of the bull going around and around the house on the hard-packed ground. They sounded as hollow and dry as the tick-tocking of a clock, measuring out the time remaining to Porfirio and Shorm. The animal had become bolder as the drought grew more severe. He had led away Porfirio's cattle, had stamped his dogs into the hillside. It seemed he and the drought were joining forces to defeat all occupation of the Santa Ritas. Only two horses were left in Porfirio's barn. The others had died from convulsive sweats caused by eating so much dry feed. But still Porfirio would not leave the place where he was born and would not lift a hand against the animal who had sometimes seemed to persecute him, sometimes to need his company.

"He is walking more slowly tonight," Porfirio said almost with affection. "Perhaps he is tired."

"Tired! Buzzards don't get tired of waiting, Porfirio!"

"Perhaps he is hungry, in truth."

Shorm joined the old man at the window. A shadow deeper than the rest moved into view between them and the barn. A horse's shrill neigh was heard, startlingly loud in the quiet night.

"By God!" cried Shorm and ran for the rifle in the corner.

Porfirio intercepted him at the door. "No!"

"Are you crazy? He's after the horses!"

Porfirio laid both hands on his shoulders and said: "You do not understand, Shorm."

In the morning Shorm said sarcastically: "I can understand this!"

The animal had somehow nudged the barn door open. There was the mark of his horn — a scratch in the worn siding. The horses were gone.

They trailed them down out of the cañon into the heat of the open valley where nothing could live long. In ordinary times they would not have gone far, but this time they were gone for good.

"Crazy, crazy with the heat," Shorm muttered, and felt some of the dry madness coming over himself. It was like a fever but worse; it was as though an irritating cloth were wrapped around him, a cloth lined on the inside with sandpaper that rubbed against him, irritating him, suffocating him, driving him half wild. When he thought about the steps of the bull going around the house in the cañon another night with monotonous regularity, he cried out: "I'm going to shoot, Porfirio!"

Porfirio said nothing.

It angered Shorm all the more. They ate their beans and jerky in silence, silently looked at the barren hillside, at the skeletons of trees and the white-hot sky where the sun, reddish-yellow, seemed to be festering. The silence was absolute, the desolation complete.

Toward evening Porfirio said: "He must be lonesome, Shorm. He keeps coming around. Did you see his tracks at the cistern?"

"I know! He's thirsty!"

"He might be."

Shorm drew all the water out of the cistern and placed it in the stone jar that stood inside the *hacienda* door. Porfirio watched. Night fell, and they waited in the darkness a long time, each on his own bunk, listening to the steps of the bull going back and forth across the yard as usual. All of a sudden there came a *snoof* at the door. Shorm jumped up. The bull was actually nuzzling at the door; his breath could be heard plainly, a series of rapid gasps like a bellows.

Shorm gave a shout. He had reached the door and saw the drought-stricken figure of the bull — the mere shell of a once noble animal — staggering across the courtyard. Thirst had brought the wild outlaw to the house.

Shorm gave a cry of satisfaction. "I'll put him out of his misery, Porfirio. You say don't shoot. You'll never say I took unfair advantage!"

He grabbed up the axe from in front of the fireplace.

"It will make you very famous!" Porfirio said, and it seemed that he must be half laughing in the darkness. "They will tell it in the bunkhouses from here to Texas on winter nights. Yes, they will sing in the plazas on Saturday nights of how Shorm made the rain . . . by killing a bull with his bare hands!"

Anger drove Shorm out of the house and down over the courtyard without another word. The bull waited for him at the bottom of the court, as if intentionally. The moonlight made the hills seem covered with a light coating of frost. It went slowly up the cañon, as if expecting Shorm to follow. He saw that it did not have the strength to go far, so he calmly put his axe over his shoulder and walked after it through the moonlight.

But the bull did not tire so soon as he had expected. Time passed. When he hurried, so did the bull. When he slowed, the bull did, too. The animal adjusted its pace to his in a manner that was a little uncanny. They went along, perhaps a riata's length separating them, penetrating deeper and deeper into the back country. The sky ahead lit up gradually as if someone were kindling a fire away off there. Sunrise came to that desolate land as it might when the world dies. This was the death of fire, not flood, as skeletons of trees and shrubs shriveled to nothing testified. So did rocks and hillsides that were stark and staring, turned lifeless. There was a pitiless emptiness of sky, a merciless punishment of light.

Shorm kept doggedly after the bull. Day had fully come, and he had not gained a step. Was he being led on? When he broke into a run, the bull did, the distance separating them remained always the same. But there was no mistaking the animal's weakness. Its hindquarters were quivering with the tremor of breakdown. Shorm knew an animal gives way first in the loin, at the base of the spine. The idea that he was actually

179

*walking down* the Santa Rita bull passed through his mind as fantastic. As Porfirio had said, it would be a legend — a tale to be told in bunkhouses on winter nights, to be sung in the plazas on Saturdays. Was the bull leading him? Shorm wiped the sweat from his face. He had come off in his fury without his hat. The sun rested heavily on his bare head.

He held the axe tightly. It was a country axe, big enough to pole over an oak or a bull. The size of it wasn't what re-assured him so much as the sight of the bull's weakness. The animal was in pitiful condition. It must collapse soon. What a fool he had been to take it so seriously!

The bull's gauntness high up in the flank under the hipbones showed lack of water. Its backbone stuck out like the ridgepole of some ruined house.

Abruptly, at mid-morning, it turned up a trail that led to the summit. There was a quickness and decisiveness about its movements that startled Shorm. Fear never quite left him after that.

Shorm gained as they climbed. He was barely a dozen steps from the bull as they went up the switchbacks in the trail, following the shoulder of the ridge, up through what had once been sagebrush and a bed of yuccas, but was now gray powder and a patch of sunburned things like porcupines half buried in dirt.

The gap between them narrowed as they reached the region of the fire pines, those curious trees whose seeds open only under the influence of a fire. They are vestiges from an age when the earth was much hotter than it is now. Only a few remain near the tops of certain mountains. No normal weather opens their cones, so they cannot seed and increase in number until a fire sweeps through the country. Then what is death to the rest of the hills is life to them.

The tongue hanging from the bull's mouth was hard and brown as the bark of the fire pines. Shorm was close enough to see that no mucous remained about its nose or eyes. The life-containing juices had dried out of the body as the sap dries out of trees. The animal was dead on its feet, but still walking. Why up? To reach a high place and die? To lure him into a trap and kill him? The sun beat down on Shorm's head with deadly force. He did not feel much anger toward the bull now. The heat haze deepened to a grayish pall as though the whole sky was filled with smoke from a distant forest fire. The air became suffocating; it was so dry and still his skin puckered. He had stopped sweating; there was nothing left to sweat. His throat hurt with dryness. His eyes burned. His tongue had swollen till it felt like a lump of foreign matter in his throat, but, as he climbed, the air grew a little cooler. A faint breeze seemed to come from far off, and he had gotten just the suggestion of it.

A stone turned under the bull's forefoot, and it scrambled to regain balance and almost fell. Shorm thought that he might make a rush and bring matters to an end. He tried to gather strength, but knew he had none. He was no better off than the bull, and the anger and the pride with which he had started were gone. The bull looked around at him. It was so close he could see into its eyes. They were feverish with pain, very round and dark with a pit-bottom darkness that had no end. That was pain. The once magnificent white horns were no longer menacing. They were bleached and shrunken, like horns seen on skulls in a desert. Pity went through Shorm for this once magnificent creature.

The summit appeared above them, bare of any growth, although in the hollow near the top was a swale of oaks, a pocket where in former years the grass had been stirrup-high to a tall horse. As they came to it,

Shorm saw that a few spears of wild oats remained in the heavier soil of the hollow and
that a few shreds of Spanish moss hung like
gray veils from the bare limbs of the trees. It
was a mournful place, doubly so for having
been once lovely. A wind passed through,
rattling the dry twigs ominously. The peak
loomed sharp above and ragged with rock.
The sky was overcast. Night had somehow
come too soon.

The bull turned suddenly and made for
him.

His panic passed as he saw how the beast
moved. It was on its last legs. It could go no
farther, so had turned at bay.

The thought flashed through Shorm's
mind that what he was going to do would be
too simple. It would be far out of proportion
to the significance of the event. Trophies
had been taken, yes, and great deeds done,
but under heroic circumstances! There
would be nothing heroic about this. A tap
on the skull. That would be all. He got
ready.

As he did so, the bull, trying to reach him,
collapsed. It sank to its knees, falling forward slowly till its nose touched the dust
almost at his feet. What fighting strength remained was summoned into its eyes and
otayed there defiantly. The last weak act was

a lunge toward him. And then the Santa Rita bull lay still in the dust at Shorm's feet.

He selected the spot between the horns, exactly in the middle of the skull, where one blow would smash out the life. Already he heard the words of the legend forming — in the bunkhouses around the potbellied stoves, in the plazas under the palm trees — of the man who walked a wild black bull to its death and smashed its life out with his bare hands.

He lifted the axe, placed it on his shoulder, and walked down the hill.

He had not gone far, when the rain began to fall. A veil of it came blowing up from the sea in a silvery-gray gust. He heard the sound of it, falling on the leaves, growing till it sounded like many tiny feet, running. The murmur of it went off across the hills like the voice of a multitude of people raised in thanksgiving. He looked back. The black muzzle had lifted and was sniffing the rain.

# THE HAPPY MAN

As soon as Blackwell's man came into the Last Saloon, we saw he was on his Christmas party. That was his trouble — trying to be happy once a year. His face wore hair, and he wore three shirts (which meant he'd been out six days), two hickory-grays and a Frisco dandy at the bottom that should have had a collar but had only a gold button in the middle of the throat. He was the stingiest man in the world, that man of Blackwell's. Why, he was so stingy he wouldn't buy the soap to do his laundry, but waited until Mrs. Blackwell did hers and then used the dirty water. All year long he never spent a dime, but at Christmas he would take a week off and go to Frisco and tie one on. He always rode back home in a taxi — we could hear it outside, purring for him to come, telling you he had plenty of money but not much time. Said he'd seen rich city folk ride past all year and hang their face at him and he wanted to see how it was done. Sometimes he would keep the cab a week, riding around, looking at things, and, when he took the notion, he would have it stopped so he could sleep, and, when a shirt got over-ripe, he would go to Abel's General Store and buy another. That was why three shirts meant he had been out a week.

But Blackwell's man didn't look happy. He passed right by us at the table and headed for the bar where Pete, our saloonkeeper, was leaning on his hand, under a blue eyeshade, thinking about Christmas.

"Howdy, Santa Claus," said Blackwell's man, "what's old Santa got for good boys that is thirsty?"

"Tom and Cherry," said Pete. "Specials." Pete was a Dane, and he sort of chewed his words, and his gray mustache in between times.

"Who?" said Blackwell's man.

Behind the bar was a mirror that reflected the suspenders crossing on Pete's back and his apron strings and the backs of all the bottles set on shelves along the mirror. Even more conspicuously it reflected a great big bowl of something hot that gave off steam enough to wet the glass and made a heavenly image, all of gold, that tilted up a little, as though this stuff were just too wonderful to stay on earth.

Pete indicated it to Blackwell's man with the smallest motion of one hand, and

Blackwell's man looked very happy all of a sudden and said: "Gimme some, Pete."

Pete filled a coffee mug and set it steaming on the bar.

They muttered over it a while, and we sat and tried to hear them, and the wind talked around the corners of the Last Saloon and didn't sound like Christmas Eve at all.

"Pete," said Blackwell's man, "it's too sweet. Gimme something to cut it . . . something sour."

Pete mixed him a whiskey sour; but, when he drank it, the lemon mingled with the sweetness of the Tom and Jerry and came out in between, like castor oil.

"Jesus!" said Blackwell's man, not looking very happy.

"Why don't you learn to mix drinks, Pete? Or get some bottles ready-mixed like Frisco has?"

He tried a shot of straight Bourbon and then began arguing with Pete and finally blew clear up and went away just as happy as he had come.

He let in wind that made us shrink and shiver right on through to our gizzards. That wind was a cross between rheumatism and a fog. It blew all the time, straight from salt marshes and the bay; and on Christmas Eve it followed Dynamite and Cherokee and me clear to the doorstep of the Last Saloon, and blew us indoors with a *whoosh* and a stomp and said: "Now, celebrate your Christmas!"

I don't know what there was to celebrate. We had to be at work by six the next morning. We worked on Christmas Day and Sunday because cattle are just as hungry then as on any other day. One of Dynamite's boys was down with the measles. Cherokee's wife was back in Oklahoma with her family. I was a young kid a long way from home. But you know how fellows get after a while — they just have to celebrate something even if they make it up.

So there we were, and we called for Pete to fill us up again with Tom and Jerry.

He came along, saying about Blackwell's man: "Poor fool . . . didn't have no coat, didn't have no hat. When he tries to buy a bottle, I tell him . . . 'No, you've had enough.' He never will be happy."

"No," said Cherokee, "not if he lives a hundred years and goes to Frisco every day."

"No," said Pete, "he'll never be happy."

"Not like we are anyway," said Dynamite. "Nobody could be happy quite like we are," and he made his blue eyes spark and his small young body shake and wiggle and become alive all over. He said: "I knowed a feller once was happy."

"Plumb happy?" said Cherokee.

"Plumb happy," said Dynamite.

"Didn't have no Sunday job?" I said.

"Nope."

"Didn't have no wife or kids?" said Pete.

"Nope."

"Well, let's hear about him," Cherokee said.

"OK," said Dynamite. "It starts back home in Utah years ago . . . feller gets off a train, important feller too, 'cause this was the Continental Comet, see, and she used to smoke through Red Jewel like a streak of light. But she stopped for him, and the railroaders gathered and yessed him up and down and cost him plenty before they was through and he could stand alone and let me see him. Now he was the unlikeliest feller you *ever* saw . . . small, pale, kind of humpy, but he had a maverick's look in his eye, and the air got away behind him when *he* moved.

"D'rectly the train took off and whipped him with its tail of dust, and he stands there, a bag in each hand, faced south across the desert towards the mountains, and never knows she's gone. Then he sees me standing there and quits his bags and comes and says

189

to me . . . 'I want to go down there.' And do you know all he done was point a hand down south?

" 'Sure,' I says.

" 'Fine,' says he, 'when do we start?'

" 'In the morning,' I says. 'I'll get the ponies.'

"So I puts him up at the Princess Hotel, M. M. Berg proprietor, and gets a hippy sorrel horse from Hap, my pard, and about then I remember all this guy has said to me, or me to him, has been yes, no . . . bang, bang.

"Next morning bright and early I and the ponies was at the hotel, and out he steps in a brand new pair of jeans and denim jumper that I knowed he'd bought from Charlie Pell across the street 'cause I could tell Charlie's denim when I seen it.

" 'Ready to go?' I says.

" 'Ready to go!' says he.

"With that he climbs aboard, and, when I seen him do it, I could tell he'd rode a horse maybe once, maybe twice.

" 'You're traveling kind of light,' I says.

" 'Yes,' he says, 'I am.'

" 'How far did you figure to go?'

" 'How far?' he says. 'Far as you like.' And he waves another hand down south . . . down where the mountains rose up big and blue. My spine begun to creep. There was stuff about this here guy I'd never seen before. Now he weren't a scientific kind, had no hammer for to bust up rocks and look inside, no nets nor bottles nor even a pencil . . . just his clothes and a silly kind of straw hat Charlie Pell had sold him. I couldn't figure it.

"I says to him . . . 'We can ride till Christmas, and it won't bother me. I know folks as will put us up at night for a good long ways at least.'

" 'Fine,' he says.

"So we took off. We rode all day across the desert, heading for the mountains that stayed always just as blue and far away, and, when I seen him ride, I knowed there was no question of this feller having ridden once or twice before . . . it was only once. The sour alkali got in his nose and made him sneeze. The new blue denim chafed his legs till they was rare as minute steak . . . I knowed . . . I could tell it in the way he set his horse, cocked forward like a little boy that's whipped and can't sit down. He never said a word. I couldn't tell if he were sad or happy or just thinking hard. We rode and rode and the sun got up and hit that desert square and bounced right back like fire from a red-hot stove. This feller's face swole up till he couldn't see the mountains he was riding for. His eyes run, and, when I asked him how he felt, he made a speech and says to me . . . 'Fine.'

"Well, I was a little whipped myself when, just at dark, we rode into Hoopaloo's place on Tank Crick out of Skull Valley. 'How far are we from the mountains now?' he says. 'We'll be there this time tomorrow,' I says, and, hearing it, he wants to look cheerful but can't because his face is burnt so it has no play left in it. He gets off kindy sudden . . . like a bag of flour that's had its bottom cut, and grabs the horn to keep from falling. I says to myself . . . 'You little son-of-a-bitch, you're game whatever you are.'

"For two days he couldn't travel, and we laid up there with Hoopaloo, eating jerky stew and beans, but what he ate made him sick, and we laid him over one day more. His face stayed raw as fire. We doctored it with bacon grease . . . with a rag on the end of a stick. It was Hoop's idea, not mine. He said it was the boss stuff for burns, though a shade salty. I bet the little gentleman could have said a good deal more about it, but he didn't. All he said was . . . 'Thank you very much, indeed!' . . . bright and sudden like a lark, and it always made Hoop jump a little.

"Come the fourth day and we rolled out

early, Hoop and I, to do the chores, and he rolls with us. 'That's all right,' we tell him, 'there's nothing much to do.'

" 'No,' he says, 'I want to help. I'll feed the chickens.'

"Later I meets him leaving the chicken yard. His face is kind of seared over now, half brown, half red, like a piece of meat on a quick fire.

" 'Did I give them enough?' he says.

" 'Yes,' I says, 'you did.'

"The yard was only ankle-deep in wheat.

" 'I'm very fond of chickens,' he says . . . damn his soul! You couldn't help but like him.

"Then we hit the trail and by noon was in a country of scrub cedar . . . little old trees ten foot high that tried to be a forest and never made it but was built just proper for their size. The little gentleman said they was like the people of the earth that was cut small out of a big pattern.

"By noon we traveled in a country that was tall and green, where water run cold out of the stone. There was meadows . . . spots of shining sun where a man would want to stop and spend his life. There were ferns and flowers and the smack of trout hitting the water after flies, everything a man could ask, but it wasn't good enough for him.

'What's on the other side?' he says.

"By four o'clock the trees was growing thinner and the rocks whiter, and I knowed the timberline was due. That would fetch him 'round, I figured. He could see from there till his eyes ached.

"We come upon a pass in a country where the trees is old before they're born and the granite lays in rocks and slabs and the rivers is no bigger than your arm. 'Over this pass,' he says, 'what is there?'

"We ride along in shadow, cold, echoing ourselves from rock and snow, and come out finally on a slope where we can see, and the sun lays still. There below us is the Twilight Country, the widest country in the world. Far to the south she goes, gray and rolling as the ocean on a cloudy day, and in her cañons are the shadows of gray heat that lie till evening. She's bare and empty as the sea, and far around her rim she seems to burn, which is the heat smoke rising. She's like a dish stuck in a fire, heaped with all the mountains of the world.

" 'That's where I want to go,' says the little gentleman.

" 'You can't,' I says.

" 'Why not?' says he.

" 'There ain't nobody goes to the Twilight Country,' I says.

"I told him of the water and the acid in the rocks, of winds that open on you like an oven door, of chambers in the stone that lets up gasses from the underworld.

" 'Of course,' he says, 'of course. I ought to go alone.'

"We turned around then and started home.

"Away that autumn word come to me in Red Jewel how a feller crossing by the Twilight Hills had found a mule, runaway mule, and d'rectly he come along himself, leading that mule, and Eben James who owns the livery stable said it was his mule . . . one he'd sold my little gentleman. Then the cry got up and come around to me as being last to see the man. 'Sure,' I says, 'I know where he is. I'll find him.'

"So I gets Hap, my pard, who can track a bird through the air, and with him four good horses, grub, bedding, canvas bags for water, and we travels and finds the place this feller says he caught the mule. It's up again' a rimrock in a cañon that was long and gray and quiet as the grave. We made our camp, and all night long the falling stones kept us awake . . . just pebbles, that's all they was, but they made you creepy, thinking the ground alive.

" 'Fore ever day reddened in the east, we

was clopping on the trail. South, we went, and south, going up that cañon while the trail roughened out and quit, and the walls rose higher till they kept our sound for minutes before they gave it back. We never heard a living noise nor seen a sign till Hap stood by a flat stone and showed me where the mule had scuffed his shoe there, coming down. A hind shoe, he said. To me it looked like maybe somebody struck a match there ten years ago.

"We worked all day to find that cañon's head. We clumb by running water that was cold and sweet, through boulders that was big as buildings and no trees. We come upon a place, and I sees the water running backwards and looks and stares and says to Hap . . . 'See that water?' And that water run *downhill!*

"Ever come along a road and see a stile built over a fence? You say . . . 'Gee whiz, Farmer Brown's built him a stile. Wonder why? Must be for something special or he wouldn't have taken all the trouble.' Well, that's how we felt that minute in that headless cañon, like some big Farmer Brown had been a-doing special things with the face of the earth and left a place for us to wander up and over, to climb on down and see.

"And what we seen!

"She fanned down gradual a hundred miles, brown and bare and stony, and far down there . . . what looked like rocks and made an eddy in her like a stone in water was really mountains. Gray walls begun on either side and reached up white to snow, and dirt flowed out of 'em like water. It halfway filled the cañons, and, higher still, them walls was colored red, yellow, orange, in a stain that rose and quit right sudden, like sometime years ago a great, big, colored sea had filled the valley just so high. Above was gray, except where slides had gashed her white, and I figured, after studying a spell, that was because the heat smoke in the summer rose and stayed right at that line of colors and made them twilights through the cañons and shut the sun off like a big umbrella, while all above was cooked plumb out to gray.

"Even now in winter the ground laid under shadow, and the sun come pale, and you kept looking up and looking up, thinking it was gonna rain, but it weren't. That was the shadow in the air, and it set your skin to creep.

"Dirt and stone was dumped in loose and helter-skelter like people dumps in piles in city lots when they're about to build, only these here piles was mountain chains. There weren't no trees nor brush nor other stuff that didn't matter or could go on later. This here was raw stuff from the beginning and, boy, believe me, you could have built the world again with what we seen . . . and had a lot to spare!

"She was too big to mention so we never tried.

"Hap says to me . . . 'Our mule passed here.' He points me out a hole where water had been once and then mud and now a kind of whitish-yellow stuff that was like concrete, only harder, and it stunk. There was rings of green and yellow 'round the edge that was the stain of acid from the rocks, and two little holes right in the center that looked like someone'd walked out there on stilts, and they was the marks of the fore-legs of our mule. 'He tried to drink here,' Hap says.

" 'He must have been a thirsty mule,' says I.

"So we kept along, and the cañons multiplied and run together and had no end and no beginning nor any meaning that was good that we could see, and Hap followed where that mule had gone like the flying birds follows the spring. We come on sudden valleys where the grass was green and water blue and always still, and all the sounds were echoes. We rode past bridges built by wind and water out of stone where God lives in the rock, as the Indians say, and casts the only rightful shadow in that land, and, when we seen His shadow lying on our trail, we chilled, picked up, and hurried through.

"At night we heard a noise like somewheres far away a furnace door was open, and next morning, if we passed that place, we'd find the little birds all dead beside the trail and see the palest shadow going on the hills for miles, and that was where the wind had cut the stone.

"There was no sound by night or day we'd ever heard or liked, till one morning in the early darkness I heard a rooster crow. 'Hap,' I says, 'wake up!'

"It come again.

" 'Jesus,' he says, 'a rooster!' . . . and buries his head.

"I says . . . 'Don't be a fool. Our little gentleman was fond of chickens.'

"Right over a hummock in a valley that was green as spring, by water as made all the noises of the sea, we found his camp. New grass was coming on it. The willows of the table had begun to sprout. His bed was puffed up mealy by the rain, and on a cedar stump this rooster set and give the sun hello.

All around him, hen folk scratched and bustled after early worms and never heard a word.

"Hap says . . . ' 'Pears like he ain't gathered many eggs of late, that little gentleman.'

"And Hap was right. He looked and looked, but this here trail was one he couldn't follow, and some place, though I couldn't say right where, it led up in the sky, I knowed.

"Then we traveled and went out the way we'd came, and, as we passed them rocks and steeps, we had a feeling like the shutting of a thousand doors, and, when we got to Red Jewel, the people that had been so hot for us to start had plumb forgot we'd gone. As for the little gentleman's folks, they never showed . . . they never gave a damn . . . they was no good . . . and the Continental Comet, she run through Red Jewel like a tongue of flame, as she does still, and never stopped again. . . . No, sir," said Dynamite — which meant his story was over — "she never stopped again."

We came back to the Last Saloon altogether in one breath, our eyes meeting as we drew it in and our feet scraping the floor, remembering how cramped they were and tired.

"He left nothing?" Pete said.

"Nothing," said Dynamite.

"What made you think he was so happy?" said Cherokee. "Why?"

"Why?" said Dynamite. "Well, I don't know . . . I used to wonder why myself. He never was a happy man to see. And then I figured it was this . . . he'd pitched his camp in the country he liked best and never had to break it up."

We thought on that some time while the wind pecked and whined around the corners of the Last Saloon.

"Maybe so," said Cherokee, "but me . . . I'd settle for a lot less than he done. If I could lay a-bed on Christmas morning, I think I'd settle for that."

Pete said: "Same with me, too."

"Well, fellers," said Cherokee, stretching himself, "six o'clock will be here soon. We'd better move."

We said so long to Pete and went outside and drove away in Cherokee's 1924 Dodge touring car, with the wind hammering the isinglass and the faintest kind of light coming on the fields that would soon be Christmas.

# THE WIND OF
# PELICAN ISLAND

From outside the bunkhouse, far into the night, we heard a sound as though a kettle were boiling on some distant fire.

"Don't care much for that sound," old Rube said. "That's the kind of wind talks to cattle."

We edged our boxes nearer the wood stove, and Dynamite said to Rollo Jane: "Rollo, tear up that box and throw it in the fire. You Okies is used to sitting on the floor."

Rube continued: "Like I told T. S. Ordway this morning 'bout them Mexican steers you fellers drove. 'T.S.,' I says, 'you got the biggest feed yard in the West. You been feeding Herefords and Durhams for years, but these here just ain't feed-lot cattle. How do you know they'll eat? How do you know what ailments they'll take? These cattle is from the old longhorn strain, and you can't predict 'em.' 'Well, Rube,' he says . . . you know how slow he goes when he's thinkin' a lot . . . 'well, Rube,' he says, standing there all duded up in felt and tweeds, 'maybe they oughta go on pasture first till we see how they gets along.' And that's how come him to call the barges and you fellers to be over here on Pelican Island."

I said — "Thanks, Rube." — and shivered.

The bare boards of the bunkhouse didn't begin to stop that wind. They simply focused it along their cracks until it struck us like a beam of ice. The kerosene lantern smoked and flared and ran a dirty shadow on the wall; the wind rustled old copies of the San Francisco *Examiner* on a table by the window, and brought us the damp, decaying odor of the delta island.

"Rollo," said Dynamite, "did ye hear me speakin' to ye a while ago?"

He and Rollo were friends, although Rollo had been a dirt farmer and drove a tractor in the yards at $3.65 a day, and helped us only when we had a lot of cattle to move. Next him by the stove sat Sims, the perfectionist, the artist on horseback. He rode his saddle like a bronze statue. Then came Reuben Child, the old Texan longhorn who had been one of Ordway's cow foremen till he fell from a truck and broke his hip. Now he said: "You fellers is too green to be this far from timber. If you want wood on Pelican Island, dig a shovelful of ground."

"Hear that, Rollo?" said Dynamite.

"Shore 'nuff," said Rollo mildly and never moved.

Dynamite rose and went outside, letting in a swirl of wind that sent doors slamming through the house and nearly ruined the lamp. Again we heard the faraway sound, a tiny, shrill note, as though a mosquito were angry or a fly had gotten caught somewhere in a spider's web.

"Don't care much for that sound," said Rube.

Dynamite came back with both hands full of dark, brown earth, kicked open the stove, and dropped in the dirt. He turned the damper till the flames roared up the black pipe. "Now, damn you, you wise old man," he said to Rube, "if this don't burn, we'll take that crutch of yours, and it will!"

"Smell it?" said Rube.

A smell like that of greasy leaves burning on damp ground filled the room.

"Whew," said Dynamite, "smells to me like somebody needs a bath."

Rollo Jane looked into the stove and said, letting his voice fade away like a little child's and die: "She's just a-burnin'. . . ."

Sims said: "What a hell of a way to spend Saturday night, watchin' the ground burn." He reminded us we were spending this night away from home on a windy island in a marsh with a cold supper inside us, and why we were. He said again: "Wait'll Ordway hears his ground will burn. He'll have a way to make money on it."

T. S. Ordway had bought thirty-nine cars of Mexican steers. When we had trailed them from the station to the feed yards, he had stood by the door of his big Lincoln sedan and never said a word. T. S. Ordway lived in that car. His office was the back seat. In it he drove thousands of miles each month between his various ranches, banks, and office buildings that were as common through the West as sagebrush and dry river beds. Men said of him that, if Western Union had an office in the town, T. S. Ordway had one. But he was his own main office. He did the business himself, and, when he got out and stood beside the car, with the hair turning a little wispy under his city hat and the skin loosening from his rock-bound jaw, he was still all man — all the way up. He had watched us pass without a word and, before half the cattle had gone by, gotten back into the car, and told the chauffeur to drive away.

We had put the steers on barges and had run them down the slough into the river and up another slough to Pelican Island. When we had trailed them down the levee road, Dynamite and I had been in the lead, and the cattle had followed, as orderly as soldiers. Modern stock would have been all over the place, but these old critters just put their heads into our ponies' tails and trudged along.

They made a queer sight — all sizes, shapes, and colors, but most of them were pintos, black and white, and there were also many solid blacks, descendants of the vicious Spanish cattle that once ran along the Río Grande. For shipping, they had been dehorned six inches from the head: only the stumps were left, big around as your wrist, but you could imagine what those horns had been.

We had trouble on Little Betty slough that crosses the island as a kind of outlying defense against the marsh. On one side is a field of young grain, on the other a wilderness of reeds and ponds — a foreign land, lying beyond water. Here, no matter what the season, it is always earliest spring. The wiry grasses, the clumps of low growth that look risen from the bottom of the sea, have in them every color of green. Kildees run crying over the mud flats; ducks go silently in squadrons down the sky. Everywhere there is an almost inaudible squashy noise, as of someone walking on a damp lawn. Every sound is in a minor key, and no color is quite true but shades into some other, suggesting, promising. This is the unknown land where life moves in water as at its beginning, and overhead the north wind blows and makes the grass stems sing like wires and brings small clouds upon the sky that lie close together and overlap, like feathers on the breast of a bird.

The marsh is a strange thing, but it was the field of grain that gave us trouble. A drainage ditch six feet wide and seven deep separated it from the road and was full of water; hungry steers trying to cross fell in and swam along until we snagged them with our loops and dragged them out. My pony, old Barb, and I had a bad time with a big yellow steer. We played him like a giant trout to a low place in the bank, and then, when I turned old Barb sharply away and stung him to make him hit that line, a horn stuck in the bank, and Barb hit the end of that rope and went straight in the air, like a dog at the end of a chain, and came back over. I felt him coming and got away in time. We rose together, sticky with mud, and he looked at me as if to say — "You got us into that." But on the next try we snaked out our fish. We had to do this several times before we reached the pasture that covers all the western part of the island. There is good feed on it and a nasty bog called King Tule on the west side toward the bay, but ordinarily cattle won't go there, and, if Rube hadn't talked to old T.S. about these Mexicans being so unpredictable, we could have come home and had our Saturday night. As it was, we went to the bunkhouse of the farm crew, and the only good thing we found there was Rube himself, who had followed us in his pickup truck like an old dog on the scent. Everyone else had gone. So we rustled around and found some cold stew and built a fire afterward in the drafty old bunkhouse, and settled down to talk ourselves into a better mood.

And now Sims had spoiled it. Sims was a kind of sour apple anyway. He said: "Nowadays it takes money to make money. If I had what Ordway got, *I'd* go to El Paso and buy *me* thirty-nine cars of steers at six cents a pound, and I'd lay 'em in here at seven, hold 'em four months, and let 'em go to the butchers at ten. That's business."

"Sure," said Dynamite, "good enough business for me."

Rube said: "Remember this . . . it takes a big man to make big money. Didn't T.S. build this feed yard himself out of a marsh?

Didn't he build the levees and turn the mud flats into gold? Likely he will clean up on these Mexican steers, but think of the risk he takes. What did he pay for 'em? . . . sixty thousand dollars. Stands to lose it, don't he? What if they takes sick, or the market drops, or the butchers don't like 'em? Where is he then? I tell you it needs a big man to make big money."

"God damn," said Dynamite. "I wish't I'd grow a little."

"I'll tell you a story," said Rube, "about T. S. Ordway that'll show you what I mean. Many years ago, when he was starting out in life, he took a contract as builder on a dam, a sub-contract it was, and under it he went out and bought materials and hired men. He did the job all right, finished on time . . . but when he came for his money, they gave him script instead. He never said a word. He went to town that night . . . Las Vegas, I think it was . . . and sat down to a poker game. Now up till then he'd never played a game of cards for money, but he sat down *that* night to play for money, and in the morning he got up with cash enough to pay his men. He said . . . 'I never paid my men in script, and I never will.'

"Now that's what T. S. Ordway done in Las Vegas," said Rube, and pulled a sack of

Bull Durham from his shirt pocket and began rolling a cigarette. The wind rattled the shingles on the roof, and made a thousand sighing and complaining sounds, with always at the back of them that little note, higher now and sharper, like a wasp getting ready to sting. "Don't care at all for that sound," said Rube. "Ever see wind talkin' to cattle?"

Sims said: "If you mean those Mexicans we drove today, they're too poor to listen."

"They're longhorns," said Rube. "I seen their daddies in Chihuahua when the wind come whisperin' of dust. Then they traveled."

Rollo Jane, who until now had spoken hardly a word, became excited at this mention of the wind and said: "It was wind done for me. Three year in a row it come, bringin' the dust. We'd get the land all worked up nice, put in the seed, and watch her come, and every year, when she got about so high" — he made a measurement between two fingers — "the dust took her . . . buried her there in the fields. We prayed for rain, but that feller up there sent us the dust instead."

Sims spoke now: "Like back home, when the apples get about so big" — and he made a measurement between *his* two fingers — "the cyclones come."

Dynamite opened the stove, and the wind

blew out a little puff of ashes. "Fire's dead."

Rube stretched and yawned. "Look outside, young feller. There's a whole island to burn."

Dynamite drew back his hand in a mock gesture of menace, but went outside.

" 'Minds me of one time years ago," said Rube, "a young feller from Stockton . . . I forget his name . . . went out at night to look for cattle on Rainbow Island over there, but he never come home. Next day they tracked him to the edge of a peat burn, and that was all they could do."

"Oh, these islands will burn," said Sims.

"Take Pelican, here," said Rube. "One place over in the pasture burned thirteen years till old T.S. come along with his pumps and flooded the land."

Dynamite returned carrying a small box with dirt for the fire, letting in a hostile blast of air that took the papers off the table and drew dust right out of the floor.

"See them steers?" Rube asked, and then he said: "Mercy, goodness . . . I plumb forgot to milk old Daisy Bell . . . sittin' here, gassin' with you fellers, and she and her baby out in the cold wind. You're no good!" He dismissed us with a wave of his crutch and stumped away into the night. We heard the sound of his pickup start and die out down the levee. It left us very much alone.

For a while we sat around the stove, listening to the wind whine and groan and pick away at the old bunkhouse. A board got loose somewhere and went to slamming, and always up high was that wasp, sharpening himself, getting closer and closer.

Dynamite went outside, came back, and said to Sims: "Lookie here." His eyes had become extra blue, I saw, so I went outside, too.

¹ We stood on the porch, and the wind whipped us with the moist, rotting odor of the marsh. We could see the levee clear to the landing, and everything was all right down there. Off the other way — west toward the bay where clouds running low under the moon made the fields go light and dark — we could see the silver grain, and beyond it in the pasture something was wrong. The steers hadn't lain down; they weren't feeding the way hungry cattle should. They stood together in groups of four or five, or maybe ten or twenty — you couldn't tell, they were so far away, but when the moonlight came just so, you could see their heads go up and a flicker of it running on their stubs of horns.

Dynamite said: "I don't like the look o' them steers."

Sims said: "Aw, what could be the matter with 'em?"

Rollo came out and joined us.

"Think I'll take a ride down there," said Dynamite, and went across the yard toward the barn, braced forward into the wind. I followed him and so did Rollo, and before we had our horses curried off, Sims came and began saddling his Appaloosa mare. I could tell he was mad.

When he got outside, he set the mare up and spun her like a top, as though they were in Madison Square Garden.

Dynamite, standing doing up his tie-rope, never looked around. He said to me, patting the rump of his brown nag: "This horse's got a lot of Steeldust in him." The horse had no more Steeldust in him than I had, but Dynamite liked to think so, because that was the breed of Texas ponies. Rollo opened the barn door wide to bring out his black Percheron, and the wind sucked in behind him and swept the floor clean all in one *whoosh*. He clambered up the great beast, who was just as slow and gentle as Rollo, and we started.

The wind flattened the clothes against our backs and blew the ponies' tails out all around them like the skirts of women. It pushed the clouds away from under the moon and made our shadows run before us, cut so clear that, when they crossed a ditch or board, we wanted to duck our heads. It cried and laughed and died beside us in the reeds like a complaining child, and then it would come again with a rush and a sweeping of a thousand wings, and you could hear that little note away up there, that wasp getting readier and readier.

"See what I see?" said Dynamite.

I could see cattle standing up. All over the pasture they rose, stretched, and stood together facing us, sniffing the wind.

"Well, we're here," I said, and, as if they heard me speak, that field of steers turned all together and began to move. Slowly and surely they followed down the wind toward the great bog of King Tule and Oyster Neck, that juts out sharply in the bay, and they never made a sound.

"Take your good holt," said Dynamite, " 'cause now we're gonna ride."

He leaned from his saddle and flung open a wire gate, and it was my bad luck to stay and shut it. The others went away down the field like bits of darkness blown by the wind. There was no question what to do; we had to get around the herd and beat those cattle to King Tule, and we had to do it quickly. I got aboard old Barb and set sail. The steers were walking quietly. I passed close to them; they paid no attention. I thought: *This is absurd. This isn't a stampede. These are gentle cattle walking over a pasture.*

First, I overtook Rollo who sat his Percheron like a sack of meal, drumming with both heels and swearing helplessly to see me pass, and then I got close to Sims and saw him holding in his mare, afraid of that bad ground. Barb passed him, going like Man o' War for the wire, and I felt proud. Dynamite was far ahead. How he got speed out of that brown nag was the mystery of all the world of running horses, but he got it — plenty of it. He already had turned past King Tule and flanked the herd.

A cloud covered the moon, and in that darkness the wind made up its mind to do us no good. It rose and sounded through the wiry grasses and brought that wasp down out the sky and set him right behind us. The cattle broke into a trot. They weren't excited; they were like old men going home, and a thought of Mexican deserts ran across my mind, shrouded in dust, with cattle moving shadowy as ghosts. Barb went for a *matrero,* which is what the Mexicans call a cunning steer, and sent him back toward firmer ground. They would go when you pushed them, but you had to push them, every one. A big dun three-year-old had his eye on the reeds of King Tule, a hundred yards away. Twice Barb scooped him up and put him where he belonged, but on the third run the steer dodged, Barb spun in the mud, and I heard an awful sound — a sound like somebody had taken a stick and wrapped it in a towel and broken it over his knee. And as I heard it, Barb went away under me, and I floated in air. It was a leisurely thing. I thought: *Good, I'm clear of him. This isn't bad. Now I'm going to hit on the back of my shoulder.* And then I hit.

I wasn't hurt; I didn't even lose my hat. I got up right away and saw the steer wave his tail and head for the King Tule, and then I saw Rollo bear down like a locomotive and scoop him up. I noticed cattle running all around me, close to me. I saw their shadows on the dark, wet grass. I saw the hip of a red steer that was going to hit me before I could turn, and then I felt a jar and a shooting pain. From the ground I saw Barb ten feet away try to get up, get only his head up, and then fall back. A wave of cattle shut him out. A hoof struck my ankle bone as a hammer drives a nail and sent pain clear to the thigh. I smelled a horrible, decaying odor of the ground itself, and then I saw Barb rise again, brace his forelegs, and stay sitting on his rump like a huge dog. He swiveled around upon himself to face the cattle, and his ears went up sharp and clear against the sky, like two leaves. The steers gave away before him. To me he wasn't a horse — he was an island glimpsed through the trough of the sea. Crab-fashion, on hands and knees, rolling and falling among the hoofs, I got to him, moving faster than ever in my life before, and, as I came beside him, the next great, living wave broke over us and went away on either side, as water does around a stone.

I shouted and brandished my hat. The cattle came on silently, loosely packed, so they could barely swerve and miss us. Barb's forelegs quivered. He kept putting a jerk in them to take that slack out, but, just when the flow of cattle had begun to thin, they snapped and let him down. Blood ran from his mouth where the bit had cut. I took the bridle off and watched Barb lie there, opening his mouth as the pain hit him, but I couldn't stand to see that and looked away.

Rollo Jane alone was keeping the cattle from King Tule, and how that boy did ride! I looked for Sims and saw him back on the tail of the herd, pretending to work hard, but he wasn't — he was afraid of that bad ground. The moon came out very bright, and far ahead I saw Dynamite fly over a piece of black marsh. Water from a pond he crossed shot up like silver sparks. He seemed to ride the air. And he was riding to win, he and Rollo, for with the help of Barb and me they'd bent the right flank south and pointed it for Oyster Neck. Two men there could bend her back along the Little Betty, and they were there. Rollo came down like six men upon those cattle. He was catching Dynamite, racing on the throat of Oyster Neck and a little to one side, when all of a sudden he disappeared.

But Dynamite didn't know. He dashed onto the point of land and turned the leaders. I saw him leap a ditch and then another, quickly, and in the moonlight far away it looked as though his pony had begun to buck. He turned fifteen or twenty head and circled to do it again, and then he must have seen there was no use. Behind, where Rollo should have been, the cattle streamed away down Oyster Neck. Dynamite didn't quit. He charged back across those steers and back again, making shadowy lines of them shoot from the herd, but he was one alone, and the job was too big. I could see his little nag fail, tripping once, and at last Dynamite pulled him up and stood there, making a long, dark eddy in the flow of cattle.

Those steers never had run; they flowed like water pressed by some invisible hand, as the earth rises behind a mountain stream and sends the water down. Still, if the fence held across Oyster Neck, Dynamite would win. I remembered Jim Magee, the construction boss, telling of the stout fence he had built on Oyster Neck to keep the cattle from the bluff and the bogs along the water, and down where the point of land narrowed I could see a black mass of steers damming up and knew the wires had stopped them — or was it board? I couldn't remember. Behind that dam the dark area of steers grew and grew, swirling in the moonlight slowly and more slowly, until they almost stopped; and then there came a sound ringing like a shot, and then another, and then a volley of them, and I saw the cattle release slowly down Oyster Neck. They gained in speed, frightened by the crash of splintering wood, pressed forward by the wind, running silently, with never a sound since the moment they began to move. The lead steers spread out singly on the bluff, clear against the sky, and behind them two thousand pairs of stubby horns were coming to find shelter from that wind, and in the bottom of the bay they found it.

I watched them go. I thought I heard waves breaking on a beach, and the sound grew, and the wind took it away and brought it back louder than before, undulating, alive, and then I knew it was the moaning of the cattle as they broke in waves upon the rock and died. . . .

Sims rode up to me and said: "Have a spill?"

"Yeah," I said, "I've had a spill."

Barb was quiet now, poor devil, but every so often he gave a kind of shiver as the pain took him. I asked Sims if there was a gun in the bunkhouse, and he said one of the farm boys had a Forty-Five. I pointed out where Rollo had fallen and told him to get over there. He went, loping his mare like he'd ridden on marsh ground all his life.

I saw Dynamite riding back from Oyster Neck. He didn't even look after those cattle but went off with Sims into a shadow, and I couldn't see what they were doing. After a long time Dynamite rode up to me and sat against the moon, with the wind tugging the brim of his hat, and, when he saw old Barb, I could hear him choke. He said they had found Rollo, lying with a broken collarbone at the edge of a peat burn. His horse had been too heavy to get out and had smothered. Then he looked at Barb again, and all he could do was swear a little softly and say to me: "Well, damn it, we made our ride . . . that's all a feller can do."

He started for the bunkhouse to get a car and a bottle of whiskey for Rollo, and I told him to find me a gun. Then Barb and I waited alone. The night wore away, and a rim of light came up along the east, as though out there a thousand miles somebody had kindled a fire. Everything I heard became an echo, which is what happens when you're very tired, and that made the island a queer place — as though all over it hundreds of people were trying to talk in different languages. Barb got restless and wanted to stand up, so I sat on his head. I wished Dynamite would come. Barb had his mouth open and would put one eye on me as he took a deep swallow of air. He didn't look like my horse at all, down in the rotten mud that way with me sitting on his head. I didn't want to remember him like that.

The lights of a car turned up the Little Betty, and pretty soon Dynamite came on foot. He carried an ivory-handled Forty-Five with a bright silver barrel, and said for me to hold the bottle of whiskey while he used the gun.

"Give me the gun," I said.

"No," he said, "I'll do it."

"Give me the gun," I said.

"Why, you silly kid . . . you don't know how to shoot a horse. You likely never shot a horse in your life."

I held out my hand, and he gave me the gun. As I walked around in front of Barb, moonlight reflected from the silver barrel. I thought: *What a silly gun. This is the kind of gun with which men perform tricks at a circus. I can't shoot my horse with it.* Then I whistled, and old Barb raised his head. I drew the imaginary lines from each ear to the opposite eye and pulled the trigger at where they crossed.

"Good shot," said Dynamite.

After breakfast we sent Sims with Rollo to the doctor. I took Sims's Appaloosa mare and rode with Dynamite for Oyster Neck to see what had happened. I wasn't feeling very happy. The wind had blown itself away and only a breeze, gentle as May, floated some delicate white clouds. We followed the auto ruts along the Little Betty that Jim Magee had made the summer before, when he hauled lumber for the fence, and that ran far from the place I didn't want to see. We found the fence splintered to pieces. Dynamite thought there would be crippled cattle on the rocks, perhaps some that were unhurt, and we were starting for the bluff, when a horn sounded behind, and we saw a pickup truck bouncing over the field. I thought it was Rube come to say — "I told you so." — but this time it was T. S. Ordway himself with Jacks, his foreman, at the wheel, and Jim Magee sitting on a box behind.

Jacks looked the same as ever — well-tanned leather doesn't change — but I had expected signs of concern on the face of T. S. Ordway. After all, sixty thousand dollars doesn't run right off the books every night. He sat, looking straight ahead out the windshield. He wore the same city hat and tweed coat that looked grown onto him as all his clothes did, as though he never took them off. He was talking to Jacks about a bridge he planned to build across the slough. He waved to us without interrupting himself and sat there, watching the distance, deliberately saying every word as men do who are used to having people listen. The new bridge, he said, would cost thirty-five thousand dollars, but by doing away with the barges and the ferry it would in the long run save money.

Jim Magee climbed off his seat and stood beside the truck. T.S. stopped talking and looked far away at nothing, as he always did when he had a lot on his mind, and then he said to me: "Boy, I'm sorry you lost your horse."

That made me feel better because all at once I remembered Barb had been his horse, not mine.

Now he said to Jim Magee: "Guess we'll have to build a stouter fence . . . eh, Jim?"

Jim agreed to that, but the old man said no more; he was talking to Jacks again about the bridge. "I'd like to see it made of concrete piers. They would last longer. Let's go back now and see if that bottom will take concrete."

Jim climbed aboard, and they drove away. Half a mile down the field the car stopped, and we could see T.S. and Jim stand beside it and put their heads together, looking up now and then and pointing off across the field, and we knew T. S. Ordway had thought of something else to build.

Dynamite reached thoughtfully through his pockets to find the dirty plug of tobacco he always carried, and, as he fished it out, he brought up with it the big idea for which he had been searching.

"One thing here you can be sure," he said. "You're working for a great man."

# FIRST DAWNING

That night Francisco was unable to sleep. The new way he'd determined to follow did not appear easy. But he resolved to pursue it with all the stubbornness of his obstinate nature.

His mother's repudiation of him followed by his humiliation at the hands of Buck Jenkins in the oak grove had changed something in him irrevocably. Beneath his rage and shame, a nearly dead ember from his youth had begun to glow: that desire to be united with a cause larger than himself, something great and worthwhile such as he'd once dreamed of and sought.

As a first step he decided to go in search of old Tilhini, the aged Indian wise man, friend and counselor of his youth, set aside and neglected all these years.

Lighting his bedside candle, he rose and went to his clothes cabinet. Rummaging through it, he found the garments and equipment he'd used as a young man. Here was the ancient waist net of milkweed fiber for carrying personal articles. Here were the moccasins beautifully beaded by his mother's hand. Here also was the bow of polished juniper reinforced with deer sinew that old Tilhini with his parents' encouragement — wanting their son to embody both white and Indian ways — had taught him to use.

Putting on the waist net and moccasins, tying his coarse dark hair into a knot at the top of his head, and thrusting the bone-handled flint knife through it, Francisco picked up his bow and took down the quiver made of a mountain lion's tail, that hung on the wall with the red-shafted arrows in it, and was about to leave the room when he remembered something.

Rummaging again in the cabinet, he came across a bowl containing powdered red ochre. Carrying the bowl to his dressing table, he moistened the ochre with water from the pitcher, mixing in tallow fat from the candle. Then, using his fingers, he smeared his body with red paint to protect it from sunburn.

Glancing scornfully at the costly silk shirt, fashionable velvet jacket and trousers, and the fancy shoes and tasseled leggings he'd discarded onto a chair the night before, he suddenly changed his mind and bent and stuffed them into his waist net.

Then, taking bow and quiver again, he

slipped quietly out of the dark house and made his way under the stars to the Indianada, that collection of huts by the river his parents had established decades ago as an alternative to mission Indian life. There old ways had been practiced all these years.

Finding Tilhini's hut empty, Francisco thought he might be in the sweat house nearby at the edge of the stream, its mounded surface clearly visible in the starlight, where men sometimes spent the night.

Descending into the interior of the mound by its pole ladder, he scented smoke, glimpsed coals, heard a quavery voice he recognized as coming from old Ramón, the crippled caretaker, who although bent nearly double from rheumatism brought wood for the daily fires and kept the sweat house clean so that others might enjoy meditation and conversation there.

"He is not here. He has gone into the hills!" Ramón explained, staring in silent astonishment at Francisco's garb, and instantly Francisco remembered this was the time of the summer solstice and that Tilhini had very likely gone into the back country to worship at a special shrine.

This rejoiced him because it seemed exactly in keeping with his new determination.

"Give me a handful of food, old man, for I travel a long trail!" Without a word Ramón took a handful of seed meal from his pouch and handed it to him.

Leaving the sweat house, Francisco proceeded into the wild interior, moving at a steady jog along the familiar river trail, the water singing beside him, the night air exhilarating. Soon he was among steep-sided mountains where dense chaparral came down with its fragrant odors and the loneliness and embracing silence opened his mind to thoughts almost forgotten since youth.

He recalled setting out along this path to find his uncle Asuskwa, his mother's brother, the famous leader of resistance against the invading white men — remembered finding Asuskwa in his hideaway deep in the fastness of the interior, and how their meeting ended for Francisco in bitter disillusion when he decided against embracing a cause that seemed doomed, however admirable. *Am I then out of my mind now?* he asked himself. For word had reached him of the terrible slaughters of Indians of the interior mountains and valleys by white settlers and soldiers. He was taking his life in his hands as he journeyed in that direction with what he had in mind, yet his thoughts encouraged him, too. Because the killing had not all been one-sided. The wild hinterland was a center of valiant resistance. White men's blood had stained Indian arrows, knives, and bullets. A struggle was taking place that had begun in the time of his father, the *conquistador,* in those days of first contact between native Californians and white-skinned invaders, and continued to this moment.

At midday he stopped in the shade of a giant sycamore by a deep pool where he'd fished and swum as a boy, and took a refreshing dip, ate a handful of Ramón's seed meal, and jogged on, feeling more at peace with himself than in years. With night came weariness, and he scooped a hollow for his body in a dry sandbar and covered himself with the sun-warmed sand, and the earth seemed to envelop him like a blessing.

Toward mid-afternoon next day he recognized familiar landmarks, looked up and saw the outcropping of brown-gray rock that contained the Cave of the Condors, the shrine to which Tilhini had once conducted him and where he guessed the old man might now have retired.

As he climbed the steep path among fragrant sage and prickly yucca, he saw the short, paunchy figure standing at the mouth of the huge, scallop-shaped opening. Instead of the coarse woolen shirt and trousers of a ranch hand that he usually wore, Tilhini was naked and painted red like himself, and wore the sacred ceremonial skirt of long, dark, condor feathers and the headdress of tall, upright owl and magpie plumes surrounded at the base by sacred, white down, signifying clouds and sky power. Tilhini was painting the rock. His brush of badger tail hairs moved steadily from the tiny pigment containers at his belt to the wall of the cave, and back.

Francisco remembered that the solstice activities of astrologer-priests like Tilhini were directed at placating supernatural forces, particularly those of the Sun, the Great Ruler, and the Moon, the other great eye that watches the earth, and thus were aimed at keeping the universe in balance and enabling human life to continue despite drought and pestilence and flood. Ordinary people were not supposed to approach at these times, but Francisco relied on his special relationship with his former mentor and advanced slowly in respectful silence.

He was surprised to see that Tilhini was painting not a sun disk or a moon crescent or a sacred condor, but a long, black line of settlers' wagons like those of the Jenkins family with white hoods drawn by black mules, following one another over a cliff into oblivion. Tilhini was painting to exorcise the white invader, and Francisco's excitement rose because it made his arrival at this moment seem especially propitious.

The old man turned, as if he'd been expecting him, and said simply: "You have come!"

Francisco was filled with joy by the intimate affection of this welcome and burst out: "Old Father, I have come back! I wish to be admitted again into the Indian Way! I wish to receive again from you my Indian name, Helek, the Hawk, that you gave me in my infancy and which I'd almost forgotten!" He was surprised how true and strong these words sounded. They came from deep down, like the gush of water from a spring.

"Very well, my son. I paint to preserve that way from those who would obliterate it." He pointed to his work. "The rock speaks my meaning. The Sky People may hear. But I have prepared myself for this moment over long hours and years, so that I am sure of what I say. What about you? Are you sure? I see you have brought your clothes with you."

"For special reasons, Old Father, that I may not disclose even to you. Yes, I am sure. Look at me. Do you not see someone new? I wish to take once more and for the rest of my life the Indian way."

Tilhini smiled with pleasure but also with thoughtfulness. "My son, I celebrate this moment. But let me speak truth. One does not easily reënter the ancient path. First, you must prepare yourself. Are you ready for the vision in which you may see the dream helper who will guide you into the future? It is after that vision that I may name you again and start you on your new course."

"I am ready!"

But Tilhini was not to be hurried. "Have you lain with a woman during the past three days?"

"No!" Francisco declared, since, indeed, it had been four since he'd stopped in San Luis at the home of a certain young widow.

"Have you recently eaten meat or greasy or salted foods? Such things are hostile to the blood of the dream seeker."

"Old Father, my hunger lies elsewhere! Except for a handful of meal from Ramón, I've not eaten for two days!"

Still Tilhini would not be hurried. "Suppose you spend the night in contemplation of the stars that are the immortal First People and are also the Great Ones from among our own ancestors? Ask them for guidance while your eyes remain open like theirs! And tomorrow, if you still are sure, I will prepare the dance. Afterward you may have your dream."

All night Francisco lay watching the stars. They seemed closer in the clear back country air. Some moved while he watched. Some were fixed in their wisdom. And when he prayed to the unwavering North Star, or Sky Coyote, benefactor of mankind, for steady guidance into the future, it was the first heartfelt prayer he had uttered in longer than he could remember.

Suddenly he felt transformed, renewed. And at that moment he heard the call of an actual coyote from the dark mountain side above — wild, uncanny, as if in answer to his prayer. His heart raced. He could hardly believe what was happening.

Old Tilhini on his bed of soft earth at the mouth of the cave stirred as if he sensed it, too. When day came, Francisco told him all.

"Then you are sure you wish to embrace the Indian way?" the old man asked.

"I am."

"Very well." Tilhini took from his waist

net his magical cocoon rattle. "Sit here beside me on the Earth Mother. Close your eyes. Listen, while I prepare the path."

Moving slowly around him in a circle, lifting and pressing each naked foot deliberately against the earth, Tilhini began to shake his rattle rhythmically. The rattle was made of the dried cocoons of spirit moths. Each contained a pebble that rasped against its inner surface with a peculiar, penetrating sound. Gradually the rhythmic insistence of this sound enveloped Francisco's consciousness, as he sat with eyes closed, until it seemed to represent all reality.

At last he heard Tilhini asking: "Are you ready for your vision?"

"I welcome it!" Francisco replied, opening his eyes dreamily as the rattling ceased.

He watched Tilhini take six tiny, white, wafer-like seeds of the jimson weed from the medicine bundle at his waist, place them in a small bowl of green serpentine, steep them in water from his gourd, mash them with the charm stone that hung by a thong from his neck. After tasting the mixture, Tilhini added three drops of water, nodded gravely, handed the bowl to Francisco. "This is Momoy, Mother Truth. She enables us to see past, present, and future clearly. But she is, also, death and must be treated with utmost respect. Drink, my son. Drink, then stretch yourself on the earth. And remember carefully everything you see in your dream vision."

At first Francisco saw nothing but those luminous shapes of many colors that appear when you shut your eyes tightly. Then gradually he seemed to rise and float through the air. He realized he was descending a long, dark tunnel that was very dangerous although he could not quite tell why. After what seemed an interminable journey, he emerged into a sunlit world that appeared strangely familiar, and he realized it was that long lost world of his youth and of his heroic Uncle Asuskwa. Once again he'd arrived at the secret stronghold deep in the labyrinthine heart of the interior where Indians came from all over the land for refuge and trade and exchange of news and plans of resistance; and there he saw the stocky, brown figure of his uncle, like his own, conferring earnestly with a group of chieftains, exhorting them to forget their differences, to unite and resist the invading white man. But one by one the chieftains' eyes glazed with inattention, and soon they drifted away toward the places where trade was in progress or games were being played or food eaten, until Francisco alone remained. He stepped forward, and his uncle embraced him joyfully.

"At last you have come! The quail have scattered, as you saw!" Asuskwa indicated the departing chieftains. "Soon we shall know if you are, indeed, Helek, the Hawk as you say!"

But Francisco said nothing. Because suddenly he felt damned by his white blood. And as he endeavored to explain this important point, he saw his uncle's smiling figure begin to fade into nothingness till he himself was left alone in the midst of that vast wilderness. All the great camp vanished. All the chieftains gone. He alone remained, until by desperate effort he managed to shout into the emptiness: "Yes, I am Helek, the Hawk!" And, as if by magic, he saw the figure of Asuskwa reappear and move toward him joyfully.

When he waked, he felt dizzy and nauseated. It seemed he'd been unconscious only a moment. Actually all day and all night had passed, and dawn was breaking. Tilhini, seated cross-legged nearby, was bending toward him solicitously. "Gently, my son. One returns slowly from a long journey."

Francisco smelled the smoke of a campfire. He sat up and shook his head to clear it.

"Drink this!" Tilhini held out a steaming bowl.

As he sipped the broth, Francisco felt normalcy return. Yet he remained strangely elated, wonderfully transformed.

"Tell me of your dream vision!" Tilhini's voice was gentle but insistent. The old man seemed larger than life, enhanced by supernatural power.

Francisco told all that had happened in his dream. "What does it mean?"

Tilhini nodded sagely, as if a guess had been confirmed. "It means you are the true follower of your uncle. It means the blood that flowed in him flows in you, the spirit that guided him guides you!" Tilhini's voice rose with conviction. "Like your uncle in the days of his greatness, you, too, will lead your people!"

Francisco's thoughts raced wildly. Could this be believed? Could he actually reincarnate the spirit of the legendary hero who had led the long, bloody struggle against the white men, rallied the wayward tribes, planned the massive uprising that had threatened to drive the invaders into the sea?

Before he could think further, Tilhini's voice was saying: "The Sun, our Father, is rising. Let us proceed!"

Francisco straightened himself, the sun's rays fully upon him. The seer was taking from his medicine bundle a white cord made of down from the breasts of condors and eagles.

First holding it gravely up to the sunrise, Tilhini lowered it and placed it in a circle on the earth surrounding Francisco. "My son," he pronounced solemnly, "again you are Helek, the Hawk, the far-flyer, the peerless hunter . . . ," — and Tilhini added in a different voice, one charged with powerful intensity — "the leader your people have awaited so long!"

Francisco was appalled by the enormity of what Tilhini said. In apprehension he gasped out: "Show me the way . . . O wise old man!"

Tilhini smiled enigmatically. "He who holds the secret of the world holds the power of becoming. And so, my son, I leave you to find your own path."

"But where am I to go? What am I to do?" Francisco cried, still bewildered.

But like the figure in his dream vision, Tilhini seemed to be receding. "That is up to you. I can go no further."

And even as he spoke, Francisco's eyes rested with astonishment on a faint trail, imperceptible before, that led on up the mountain above them.

# DEATH IN OCTOBER

After the death of T. S. Ordway, El Dorado Investment Company continued as before. The mill ground just as much feed; the cattle in their pens went right on eating, getting fat, being sold at a good profit; and the boys that made the wheels go around were on the job at seven every morning when the whistle blew. They earned their three dollars, but at the end of the month the pay checks came out signed, not by T. S. Ordway, but by So-and-So, trustee.

One thing the great man never failed to do through all his wide realm of ownership was to sign the pay checks personally — hundreds of them. It cost him the last week of every month, but he did not complain. "I never paid a man in anything but cash," he had said. "If I can't see his face, I want to know his name." You see, this was later in his career, when the meetings got in his way, the papers, dividends, and debentures.

After he died, the river ran on down. The days began out of the east, broke over the high Sierra, and passed on down with the river out to sea, just as they always had

239

done. The great, green delta on an afternoon swayed and muttered and lapped, as the wind played in the reeds around the islands — the islands with their levees built by Thomas Ordway, master architect, who had worked in earth, not wood or stone.

Yet after he went, there was a difference. People said so. Perhaps they looked for one; and where you seek, you find, as the Good Book says. But in the noises of the wind there was an echo as it talked across this wide city of boards and cattle; in the grinding of the mill there was an echo, a different sound when you listened. It seemed the feed trucks moved more slowly; the men stopped more often to talk. Little things made a bigger difference. When steers went off a quarter of a cent, it was generally decided that the market would not have dared to do that in the time of T. S. Ordway. When school children passed through in caravans, and on Sundays when pleasure cars lined the county road that runs along the yards, the people made no sound but looked with wide-open eyes, for this might be the last time anyone would see El Dorado Investment Company, about which everybody had heard.

In the bunkhouse, in the cookhouse, we wondered what was going to happen. During the day we gathered often at the barn to talk — the old, gray shelter, eaten by the wind and rain, that was a derelict when T. S. Ordway found it standing on a mound above the sloughs. There he had his dream and built his city out of mud and reeds, the richest land in all the world, where wealth lay in the decay of centuries, alluvium, waiting for a man who could see, but waiting not alone, as we found out.

Day after day strange cars glided up and down the alleys, filled with men in city suits, smoking good cigars — trustees, appraisers, inspectors, heirs nobody ever had seen — all of them foreigners that didn't belong. It hurt you some way just to see them. Rumors came with every carload: the yards were being sold for taxes to Swift, to Armour, to the government for an experiment in cattle like those they had made in electricity. But nobody knew.

All that summer was unusually cool. Sea fogs blew in and lay all day. On clear evenings after sunset, off westward toward the blue hills, a cloud formation was observed several times like a great, red spear thrust in the sky; and people said this was a sign, and others said it was because of the war raging far over the sea.

Archibald Jacks ran the yards as he had always done, but his shoulders drooped a little, and there was no smile in him. Reuben Child, earliest made and latest left of all the helpers of the great man, came to the barn the first few days and lingered like an old dog around the place he had seen his master last; and then he left and was seen no more. At evening his white cottage by the slough had no light; and some said he had gone away into the hills to die, and some said he had gone back home to Texas where he had been born so long ago and where he had first met Thomas Ordway.

Summer blended into fall, the lonely time of year. The days came hot and still, with a hush and everlasting echo, and the sound of wind passing somewhere up above that never touched the earth. From the ventilator on the mill dust rose and spread a fan across the sky. You could hear the heavy, hollow grinding of the gears, digesting cattle feed. . . . The things T.S. had set going kept on after him.

Daylight on those mornings found dry ground. There was no dew, no night that mattered. No wind blew, yet in the reeds there was a rattle dry as death. You could hear the endless roaring of a tractor in the fields beside the river where it dragged a great disk plow to break the ground for next year's crop, and here a shroud of yellow dust rose up and hung above the field.

On the sixth day of October the great disks ripped open an Indian burial mound, and the skeletons came up like white roots out of the ground. For a day or two there was a good deal of excitement over this, because the sixth came on a Friday, and during the week-end people from Bird Town and the nearest villages came down to collect trophies. Later all this was carefully remembered and retold, together with the facts that cats had eaten grass and for three nights straight a ring had lain around the moon. But for the moment the novelty passed and would have been forgotten except for what happened Monday.

Ten minutes after ten the anthrax struck. The first steer went down in Pen 78, close beside the water, and a little blood ran from its nose. Pen 77 was next, the steers dropping as if they had been poled over. Few lived more than half an hour. Not till afternoon did we know what they had. There had been no anthrax in the valley for fifty years. The veterinary stocked no serum; he wired San Francisco.

Old Jacks cruised around the alleys in his pickup, looking the way he did the afternoon news of Ordway's death was brought to him.

The cattle dropped like flies. All Monday night we stood and heard them moving in the dark, kicking in the dust a little when they fell, and soon all would be quiet but for the restless moving of the other cattle up and down the pens. By morning the water troughs were ringed with dead.

Then the serum came, and we went to vaccinating. All day long the columns of cattle choked the alleys, moving to the pens around the branding chute, and the yellow dust rose as it does from armies marching. There was no sound. This was the quiet death, taking some even as they moved to safety. Only the grinding of the mill went on; and the plow, breaking the land, its sound falling on the out-turn, coming louder on the way back; and over it the dust rose yellow, too.

We put the needle into better than a thousand head a day, but thirteen thousand cattle take a lot of vaccinating. The biggest, fattest ones came first — they cost the most. Around the chute there was a milling red and dusty mass, the press and clatter of the cattle on the boards, the sharp bellow of pain as the needle stuck them, and the white and silver flash of Dynamite's bare forearm with the syringe, for it was he who did the vaccinating.

"Die and prove it!" he would yell, driving

home the needle in the soft necks; and the steers would buck and squeal.

Nazi Joe was there, working the drop gate at the far end of the chute where the cattle went out when Dynamite finished them. Joe was a roly-poly, little, old German with a battered, dun-colored, felt hat, stained with sweat, that he always managed to keep jaunty on his head, cocked up a bit behind, so that he looked like a poor, Bavarian mountaineer. Actually Joe came out of Prussia, I think. He wore his shirtsleeves short, cut off at the elbows like a little boy's; his face was red from years of weathering, and his eyes were as blue as Dynamite's, only they didn't move — they stuck and stared. A Dutchman stiff and stubborn, with a streak of astrology in him, Joe had a mind that was a whiz on a column of figures, but on other things got just so far on the right track — and then off into either air or water.

Uncle Arky Billy was there, Cherokee and Sims, and Jacks himself, coming and going in the pickup, his face growing longer with the lines of cattle.

Outside in the alleys the dead wagons went about their business, hauling the bodies, chained behind in tandem, to the fields where they were piled with straw and gasoline, and burnt. Their smoke rose and mingled with the dust the tractor made, until the sun turned red and the stench of roasting meat hung in the air all day.

So it got to be the thirteenth, our lucky day, and we waited by the chute after our noon meal for Jacks to come. He said it was our lucky day; we had eleven hundred head to go, but he didn't come, and he didn't come; so we talked it over and went ahead without him, Dynamite in charge. Since Ordway died, Jacks had been like a man walking in a dream, and all the yards for him were like a great house he had known well, furnished in a way he'd seen a thousand times, every chair in place — but nobody home. You'd find him sometimes in the evening, sitting in his pickup alone by the mill or on the docks where the barges tie up and leave their sacks of grain, where the hustle and the bustle is all day, with no time to think and remember. Jacks liked to find those places after work; there was no telling where he was now, so we went ahead.

"Stack 'em up, you guys!" sang Dynamite. "Cattle, *cattle*, ten head to a chute!" And Cherokee and Sims and I shoved them in with terrible shouts, waving our gunny sacks, shaking our sticks.

Dynamite worked from a platform built

three feet off the ground along the chute. Uncle Arky Billy helped him, filling the syringes. Nazi Joe worked his drop gate at the far end. He said slowly after a while: "Jacks . . . he got zee anthrax." Joe came out of Germany in 1912; his English still had a buzz in it.

"Anthrax?" said Dynamite. "You're crazy. Men . . . *zey* don't take anthrax."

"Yes, zey do, too," said Joe, yanking down the bar that raised the gate. "Dat's just where you mistaken. Zee anthrax is one of zee most terrible diseases known to man."

"What makes you think he's got it?" said Dynamite to Joe, and to a steer: "Die, you son-of-a-bitch! Die and prove you're hurt!"

Joe kept right on; you couldn't put him off once he got track of an idea; and he never hurried and never let his voice get up or down. "Zee stars say it is his time."

"Stars! . . . stars my foot . . . stars don't talk, they shine. God dammit, Joe, you're gonna break your back out there by the cookhouse some night. I've seen you, bent like a barrel hoop."

"Zee stars never tell a lie," said Joe. "If you study dem, you would be money ahead of zee game. Take Jacks, he don't know, you see . . . October is his month. In zee first part he stand good chance for success . . . in zee middle part, especially zee thirteenth day or fourteenth, he should be careful, watch his step. Zee stars never say . . . 'You must.' . . . only . . . 'You should' . . . there is a good chance of things to happen dis way, happen dat way."

"Horse water," said Dynamite.

"Man . . . ," said Joe, "man, he is a product of zee sun. If he be born when sun is overhead, zee upright position of zee cornstalk, he has more chance for success . . . he be like a tide coming in. But October is not very good month . . . sun is changing . . . he is tired. You find a quarter shadow around noon. . . ."

"I bet you Jacks ain't got the anthrax," said Dynamite. "What makes you think he has?"

Sims piped up: "I seen a black sedan parked by his house at noon."

"Doctor Hartley's car," said Joe. "Jacks went into his room before lunch, lock zee door, don't let nobody in. They telephone zee doctor."

"You've been listening to that Thelma Jenkins's talk," said Dynamite. "I seen her coming to the cookhouse after noon to get her eggs and butter for old lady Jacks. You'd better not listen to her . . . she'll have you b'lieving stars is stripes before she's through."

There was no talking while Sims and I and Cherokee crammed home another chute.

"Anthrax is zee most terrible death," said Joe. "One time on Two Street, Sacramento, last April ven I vas dere, I talked vid a fellow who has only one eye . . . half his face vas cut away . . . you know . . . big scar. 'Vat's de matter your eye?' I says. 'Oh,' he says, 'I hadda anthrax.' 'How does dat disease operate?' I says. 'Very simple,' he says. 'Anthrax of zee human being is de most terrible disease. Once de germ is in de blood, dere is no hope . . . only chance,' he says. He says he owns a bunch of cattle, one of dem die . . . him and anudder fellow, dey chop it up, zee knife slip, cut him on de hand, and dat vas de way zee germ obtain entrance to zee body. Dey rush to a doctor . . . doctor, he say . . . 'Can do nudding . . . first we must follow zee germ.' He put him on de table, under zee X-ray. Venever zee germ come near surface of zee blood, zey try to catch him. If he come to zee heart . . . too bad. Zis time dey have good luck . . . he come out in zee eye, and zey catch him with a knife."

"God Almighty," said Dynamite, "I hope they don't do that to old Jacks."

249

"Maybe so, maybe not," said Joe. "Maybe he die. Remember der is nudding accomplished but vat der is destruction first."

Joe kind of had us there, and we thought a bit about many things, and Sims said half aloud: "Jacks cut his hand this morning . . . on that steer, remember? He was cutting the screw worm out of its back."

Jacks *had* nicked his hand; we all remembered.

"Once zee germ has entrance to zee human body," said Joe, "a man is gone. Dat is why information of zee stars is useful."

"The stars don't know that much," said Dynamite. "There ain't nobody knows about death . . . only God Almighty."

Joe didn't answer. When he wanted to call you a liar, he could do it with the back of that blunt head of his, he was that stubborn.

"No, sir, Joe, you're full of hop and star dust," Dynamite went on. "Death ain't in the sky . . . death . . . death's like a lariat rope, and you're on one end and God, He's on t'other. You're born thataway . . . strung up . . . and that way you run your life . . . like I've let many a steer go along after I had him roped, till I found a place to bust him out . . . and then I took my dallies and made my pony squat and hold. Same with death . . .

you have your run and take your spill. Ain't it so, Uncle Billy?"

"That's right, Dyney boy," the old Arkansawyer said. "Yes, sir, that's about it, I reckon, for the most part. We're on one end, God Almighty, Lord of Jacob, He's on the other. Reckon he had time to repent?" said Uncle Billy. "Jacks, I mean. He weren't much of a church-going man, you know."

"Oh, I think he would," said Dynamite. "Jacks's heart was in the right place, though he could be ornery, the old son-of-a-gun. Many's the time I've wanted to warp his head with a neck-yoke. But I reckon, if he has took off, he's up there now a-lookin' down on us boys."

"Sure hope so," said Uncle Billy. "*Sure* do."

Cherokee said: "You boys is sounding mighty highfalutin' in this here argument, like you'd all been to college. Seems to me this death come right out of the ground."

Cherokee didn't often say much, but he made sense when he opened his mouth. We took a look around our feet, and I remember it was quiet just then, between two fillings of the chute, and you could see the tower of dust built by the plow and hear the tractor going faintly; and then, in a second, we got fear. Nobody said so; we just had it. It ran quicker than any disease; and we were looking at our hands for cuts and shifting on our feet without intending to, as though we stood on something hot.

Up Long Alley by the mill the boys were bringing us more cattle, the last ones, and their dust in the air looked worse than poison gas.

"Well, I dunno," said Dynamite, but his heart wasn't in it. "Cattle," he hollers. "Whatsa matter with you guys? Gimme some cattle." He grabbed a syringe from Uncle Billy and rolled his right sleeve up a notch as though he was ready for the anthrax then and there, by God.

We began to move slow motion.

Two trucks came up empty from the mill, whining on the turn of the road and passing us right by as they did a hundred times a day, but this was different — it seemed as though they were running from something.

"Here's your wife, Dynamite," said Sims.

The top-heavy Packard sedan rolled down the slope from the barn and made the dust burn with its brakes. Maxine got out. She was in a hurry; there was a handkerchief across her face.

She ran and jumped up on the fence and leaned our way, and she was screaming mad. "Don't any of you men come home!"

she yelled. "Not one, not any one of you . . . Sims, Annabelle told me to tell you . . . and Cherokee, your Mary says the same . . . it's *anthrax!* . . . Jacks has it! . . . he locked the door, wouldn't let them in, but they took the axe. No!" she said, seeing Dynamite start toward her. "No," and it made your spine go cold to hear it, wife to man. *"Stay back!"*

Dynamite went all the faster.

Maxine was off that fence and into that car quicker than the light of day. She put her head outside and called back once: "You can't come near the babies . . . don't you *dare!"*

Dynamite stopped at the gate, looking after her and cussing.

Sims started to run.

"Where-ya-going?" Dynamite's voice would have taken off your ear.

*"The dust!"* screamed Sims.

Dynamite knocked him down, and he rolled in the dust.

Cherokee said: "Say, Dyney . . . reckon we outta stop that plow, and them trailing cattle down the alley there? Don't you reckon we outta stop them just a while till we get all this straight?"

"We ain't a-stoppin' nothin'," said Dynamite.

Sims got up and looked like he wanted to run again, but Dynamite said to him: "There'll be no running while I'm here, understand?"

"Listen," said Uncle Arky Billy, "listen, boys!"

We looked into the sky. There was no wind; the sun up there was red and evil as the heart of a boil. We listened, but the sound we tried to hear had gone. "The mill," said Cherokee. "She's quit."

"We ain't a-quittin'," said Dynamite.

"It was the plow made the dust," said Sims, half whimpery.

Now that the noise was gone, it seemed the air had died like a body does when the blood goes out of it. All those alleyways and mangers, all that valley, river, and the hills beyond were empty veins of air, and only the cattle moved or made a sound. Two were dead just beyond us in the holding pen, Bar-Seven steers.

Hank and Jerry, who'd been helping out there, had taken off. I saw them hurry out the back way behind the scales, up toward the barn. Uncle Billy filled a syringe, matter-of-fact as biscuits and ham gravy. Nazi Joe tightened up a little in the face, but he stuck to the handle of his drop gate, ready for that destruction he'd talked about.

"Lookie," said Dynamite, and his voice picked us up.

Gliding low, cruising down the alley from the barn, a pickup truck was coming in just the easy way Jacks always drove.

The little truck stopped by the outer gate; the door opened, and a man got out, but it wasn't Jacks or even his ghost. It was Reuben Child, whose day was gone, whose face was like the side of a mountain where the rains have been. "Howdy, fellers," he said. "Vaccinatin'?"

He hobbled over; he needed a cane to walk. "Understan' ye got the anthrax in your herd," he said, and hardly got his voice above a little girl's.

All his strength was in his face and eye, but he made you want to knock down mountains, that old Rube. "Just thought I'd lend a hand," he said. "Not doin' much these days."

We began to vaccinate.

"Haven't seen you lately, Rube," said Dynamite. "Where you been?"

"Me?" said Rube. "Oh, here and there."

He was looking mighty fit for a man who's just been here and there. Those wide, gray eyes, always finding some horizon, had got hold of one they liked, and it had lit him up inside in a way we'd never seen. If Rube had been a drinking man, I'd have said he'd taken a few.

He held the syringes; Uncle Arky Billy, who although he had good legs under him like old Rube would never see sixty again, got out behind with us into the crowding pen; and then even Sims was ashamed and went to work. We crammed those cattle through. The dust rose up so thick you really couldn't see. Your face turned black; your hollers turned to croaks. We used up all the water in the bottles and didn't dare take the time to send for more.

The anthrax never slackened. It stole the cattle out from underneath our sticks. Here a heifer, there a steer — down like a hog with an axe on its head, then a twitch, a little blood. We let them lie, forgot about the dead wagon not coming. The boys brought the last pens of cattle up Long Alley and took off without a word, drifting in the dust like shadows, but we never cared.

All of a sudden it got very dark. The wind that for two weeks had wandered up there trying to get down came now, and the dust was made up into sheets and spirals and went everywhere. The wind stopped; the dust cleared off; and there was the sky all brown and rotten as though the wind had gone up there with all its dust. The first rain brought thunder. Then the sky broke open.

We wallowed in it, thankful at first, till we saw the mud sticking and thought of germs that live for fifty years, and then I think some of us would have prayed, if we could, or had had the time. But things were happening. The cattle couldn't make the chute. The slick board bottom, polished by their hoofs, greased with the mud and dung, was no good footing. They went down; they stacked up on one another. A little heifer broke her neck. We spent twenty minutes clearing out the chute, while thunder smashed the hills across the river, and the raindrops hit us big as dimes.

Rube called it off. "There's one place we can go," he said, waving his cane toward the barn.

"Not with all these cattle," said Dynamite. "What good will it do? This here's the only chute."

"We'll use our loops," said Rube, "if we ain't forgot quite how. Otherwise, these little cattle won't make it till morning. We only got two hundred left."

So we turned the others into the holding pens and took our two hundred little Double Arrow steers and drove them to the barn. We made the horse corral a holding pen. We cleared the inside of the barn all across one end, moved the bales of hay, dragged an old harvester, kicked out some mangers so there was room to move between the walls from one side to the other, across thirty yards of dirt. This was our crowding pen.

We lit the lanterns and brought the little steers inside, a bunch at a time.

Rube said to Dynamite: "Get me your horse."

"Hell, Rube," said Dynamite, "better let me do the roping."

"I'll do her," the old man said.

We helped him onto Dynamite's renegade nag that might have got a pint of Texas Steeldust in him generations back. He hurt Rube; that broken hip hadn't been in a saddle for ten years, but the old man straightened himself up bit by bit. He wanted to do it. There was something about Rube this night we all remembered — a rising in him and a kind of light, and he moved clean-cut out of the air, smoothly, like he knew just where he was going.

Dynamite whispered: "Rube's sure ridin' high. What's the matter with him? What's he got?" But at that time I didn't know myself.

He took his stand, old Rube, halfway along the mangers from the little steers, where they'd have to run between him and the wall, and began to build his loop, did it from the wrist, with a flick over and a flick back, and gave the signal down the barn for the boys to let the cattle come.

The wind blew the lantern light all cock-eyed, splashed it on us, and rocked the barn and made the floor smoke dust.

Rube sat his horse. From Canada to Mexico his name was known — hardly a brand that hadn't felt his loop in olden days, Hooleyann or straight, and no maverick that ever ran was quicker than his hand and eye.

Dynamite and I stood back; Cherokee cut and pushed a little steer and let him scamper down the wall, under the lanterns, harness, and old blankets.

The hempen loop ran out like light, spun underhand, and ringed the yearling with a gentle slap. Rube had his dallies fast before the animal took a step. Dynamite put a loop on both hind-legs. I shot the syringe in the soft neck, handed the gun to Arky Billy, loosened Rube's rope, and pulled it off.

"That weren't so good," said Rube. "I meant to lay a figure eight."

Next time he did, and the animal stepped through with right forefoot and tied himself. Rube set him down without so much as a finger's help. And so on with the next, and the next. Once we took a rest; once Rube missed a loop. Other than that, every throw but half a dozen was a perfect figure eight; and Dynamite, on the ground waiting, had only to shake his head and smile, or lay down his rope to help me.

The two hundred-odd head took us so far into the night that we never knew how long it was.

The storm kept us company — and the tromping of the cattle, the rustle of the running loop, and the squeak and rubbing of Rube's saddle when his pony took a squat and laid the critters down.

The old man never showed his pain. The hours wore away and made him young. He took off the blue denim jumper and tightened his silver-studded belt, a prize from some rodeo long forgotten, and with the work he straightened in the saddle till the patient smile we always knew him by had gone and he wasn't bearing something any more — he was doing it himself.

I wish I could tell just how he looked. Nobody could who hasn't seen a man inside his job or a woman with a child.

We finished, and the little steers that had begun at one end of the barn were all crowded at the other.

"Turn 'em out," said Rube. "Let the rain have 'em. The anthrax never will."

We sat along the bench by the door where the boss' saddle hangs, along with some pairs of extra stirrups, a couple of bits, and a strip of hose for ramming down the throats of critters when they choke.

"Death?" said Dynamite to Rube, one eye on Nazi Joe. "You sure beat him out of that one, Rube. Your loop is quicker than the Evil Eye."

Rube was tired; he smiled now the old way.

"Hurt your hip any?" said Cherokee.

"Little," said Rube, "but shucks, just shows what a feller can do when he wants. I should have been on a horse years back."

"How come . . . ," said Dynamite, "how come ye took to it tonight?"

"Oh, I dunno," said Rube, lifting his Stetson and wiping his high, white forehead where the sun never reached. "I dunno . . . I guess because I had a dream."

"A dream?" said Dynamite.

"Yeah," said Rube. "Funny, my old daddy had one like it years ago, spring of 'Ninety-Two, I think it was, or 'Ninety-Three. We trailed 'em from the Pecos to Wyoming, two thousand longhorn steers and Dad and me and eight good boys.

Crossed the Republican River on the first of May. That night we bedded on a grassy knoll by water where the bluestem went for miles knee-high to horse and man. We bedded just at dark after a long day and laid the wagon tongue for the North Star so we could find the morning's trail.

"I remember how old Tigue, the cook, got out his Dutch oven that night, wiped it with his special cloth made of a flour sack, and baked us bread . . . bread and beans and jerky stew. We lived like kings.

"Dad dreamed that night. Some way he was in a house alone, a room all bare but warm. It was late afternoon, 'bout four o'clock. From where he sat there was a window and a quarter-angle view up a long rise to some blue hills where night was beginning to gather and creep down. That ground was funny, too. It was all bare, low brush and stones.

"He set quite a while, he said, wondering why nobody come, and then he realized that house was empty, bare and empty as a house can be, yet full of yellow light . . . the afternoon, you know. And as he set and got his view out quartering from the window in a long slice up, it seemed he just couldn't quite see enough, that just around the edges of that window was the home he knew . . .

the green alfalfa patch, the orchard trees, the good, red barn and horses standing, the windmill pumping water . . . *ker-blong, ker-chug, ker-chug, ker-blong* . . . and the spatter from the leaky leathers as it hit the stones.

"There was all this goodness just on either side of where he looked, but that slice of ground he had to see . . . it was just a desert, bare as anything, with night creeping down along it 'mongst the little stones.

"Seemed like the sun'd set already, he says, but he couldn't figure it, felt sure it was just four o'clock, half day, half night.

"So he set. He waited a long time, said he never did know why . . . wanted to get up and look around the edges of that window and see all the good things he heard and smelt and knew was there . . . but he just couldn't do it. Said he began to listen for something, something special, and then he heard it coming on the walk outside, crunching in the gravel step by step, heard the door open and latch shut and the jingle of spurs hung on the buckhorn by the wall.

"And then he said he *knew*, and he felt happy. D'rectly the steps come near and give him leave to look, and there stood his old daddy, and his face was all one smile like he was powerful glad to see his son again. He touched my daddy's shoulder and just

263

says . . . 'Howdy, Son.'

"This was the dream my daddy had that night," said Rube. "At daylight we moved on. In seven days he died, and far in old Wyoming, on the Crazy Woman beyond Ten Sleep, we laid him in the ground."

Rube stopped talking, but outside the wind kept on, lightly now, with a good deal of rain in it. The gusts caught water falling from the gutter that runs along the eaves, and hammered it against the barn one second and let it slosh on down the next. Rube began rolling a cigarette. He never used two hands. We watched him roll and lick and smear the tangled weed and paper, then hold a match until it glowed.

"That was the dream you had?" said Dynamite.

"That was the dream I had," said Rube. And after a while: "Well, reckon I'll call on Jacks before I go along. He's poorly . . . took the chicken pox, you know."

# ABOUT THE AUTHOR

Robert Easton was born in San Francisco, California. In one way or another all of his work has been centered on the history and people of the American West. His first great critical and popular success was THE HAPPY MAN (1943), a portrait of California ranch life in the late 1930s. *The New York Times Book Review* said of it, "Good writing of a kind that is difficult and rare," and *The New Yorker* stated that it has "a clear narrative style and a sure sense of authenticity." Easton went on to write MAX BRAND: THE BIG "WESTERNER" (1970), a biography of Frederick Faust, and recently with his wife, Jane Faust Easton, edited THE COLLECTED STORIES OF MAX BRAND (1994). After three decades of research, his epic Saga of California began with THIS PROMISED LAND (1982), spanning the years 1769-1850, and is continued in POWER AND GLORY (1989) and BLOOD AND MONEY (1998). Since THE HAPPY MAN there can be no doubt of Robert Easton's commitment to the American West as both an idea and as a definite and distinct place. Beyond this, in all of his work he has been guided by his belief in what he once described as a writer's concern for "the living word — the one that captures the essential truth of what he is trying to say — and that is what I have tried to put down."

We hope you have enjoyed this Large Print book. Other Thorndike Press or Chivers Press Large Print books are available at your library or directly from the publishers.

For more information about current and upcoming titles, please call or write, without obligation, to:

Thorndike Press
P.O. Box 159
Thorndike, Maine 04986 USA
Tel. (800) 223-1244 or (800) 223-6121

OR

Chivers Press Limited
Windsor Bridge Road
Bath BA2 3AX
England
Tel. (0225) 335336

All our Large Print titles are designed for easy reading, and all our books are made to last.